Zafir slid his hands over hers.

Fern tried to look away, but he was tall and very close. He smelled good. Earthy and sweaty, but not overpowering. Masculine and intriguing. She'd never met a man with such an air of command. Zafir was in his prime, not just healthy, but radiating supremacy.

In the back of her mind, she knew she was behaving like a rock-band superfan, speechless in the presence of a man with star quality, unable to move, but he was so incredible. She found herself staring into his eyes for too long. She knew it was too long, but she couldn't look away from those crystal blue-green depths. They quested, delving into hers, demanding something she didn't even understand.

Say something, she thought, and let her tongue wet her lips.

His gaze lowered to her mouth.

Her breath evaporated.

She found her own gaze dropping to his mouth and wondered how it would feel to have those smooth lips rubbing against hers. Her heart was fluttering like a trapped bird, her pulse pounding in her ears.

He lifted his hand to hover hotly next to her cheek, scorching her. His brows jerked in some type of struggle. *Was he going to kiss her?*

Seven Sexy Sins

The *true* taste of temptation!

From greed to gluttony, lust to envy, these fabulous stories explore what seven sexy sins mean in the twenty-first century!

Whether pride goes before a fall, or wrath leads to passion that consumes entirely, one thing is certain: the road to true love has never been more enticing!

So you decide:

How can it be a sin when it feels so good?

Sloth—Cathy Williams

Lust—Dani Collins

Pride—Kim Lawrence

Gluttony—Maggie Cox

Greed—Sara Craven

Wrath—Maya Blake

Envy—Annie West

Seven titles by some of the most treasured and exciting Harlequin Presents authors!

The Sheikh's Sinful Seduction

Dani Collins

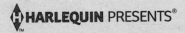

ISBN-13: 978-0-373-13799-2

The Sheikh's Sinful Seduction

First North American Publication 2015

Recycling programs
for this product may
not exist in your area.

Printed in U.S.A.

www.Harlequin.com

Canadian **Dani Collins** knew in high school that she wanted to write romance for a living. Twenty-five years later, after marrying her high school sweetheart, having two kids with him, working several generic office jobs and submitting countless manuscripts, she got The Call. Her first Harlequin Presents book won the RT Reviewers' Choice Award for Best First Series Romance. She now works in her own office, writing romance.

Other titles by Dani Collins available in ebook:

With a theme like lust, well, duh. Of *course* this one's dedicated to my husband, Doug.

Friends, and even strangers, love to waggle their brows and lower their tone to a suggestive level and ask romance writers, "How do you research your love scenes?" Here I'd like to officially give my husband the credit he deserves. He's always been extremely patient when I bring the laptop to bed so I can take notes. Thanks, honey.

CHAPTER ONE

ARRIVING AT THE oasis brought Fern Davenport back to life in a way she'd never experienced. The two-day camel trek through the dunes that she had anticipated with such excitement had been exactly what her employer and friend, Amineh, had warned it would be: a test of endurance.

But worth it. Exactly as promised.

After nothing but shades of blinding white and bleached yellow and dull red, the glimpse of greenery had Fern sitting taller, bringing her nose up the same way her camel did, searching for the scent of water. As they entered the farthest reach of the underground spring, where the palms were stunted and the grass sparse, she felt like a giant looking down on the tops of trees. The sun was already behind the canyon wall and blessedly cool air began to slither beneath the flapping edges of her abaya to caress her bare legs.

The tension of fearing for her survival began to ease. She wanted to release a laugh of relieved joy.

Outbursts of any kind weren't her thing, though. She preferred to be as invisible as possible. Fern considered herself an observer of life, not so much a participant, but for the first time she experienced something like what a frisky lamb or a cocky adolescent must feel. It was a strange awareness of being alive. Her blood cells took on new energy and her pulse returned to vigorous beats. She wanted to throw off the weight of her clothes, expose her hot skin to the verdant air, kick up her heels and soak life through her pores. She wanted to be one with nature.

Awash in this state of renewal, she looked ahead to the clearing where the caravan would unload and saw *him*.

Just a man in a *thobe* and *gutra*. He could have been one of the camel keepers for all she knew, but a deep, feminine part of her recognized the kind of male that called to any woman. A leader. One whom other men looked to for direction and approval. Confident. A man of strength whose muscles strained the white tunic that draped his shoulders. He wore sandals and his feet were dusty, but he planted them firmly. With ownership.

She forced herself to lift her gaze to his face, barely able to withstand the impact of such handsomeness. How could a man be so beautiful yet so rugged? He was a product of the desert, she supposed, cheeks hollow and roughened by stubble, skin deeply tanned by the sun, mouth somber yet sculpted and…how did she even sense this? *Sexual*. A hawkish nose and brows as straight and firm as the horizon and then…

Green eyes. As startling and revitalizing as this oasis.

His sheer magnificence took her breath.

"Uncle!" the girls cried and the man's severe expression flashed with a smile that made wistfulness bloom in Fern's chest.

Men were such puzzling creatures to her, having mostly been passing ships in her life. She'd attended an all-girls school where even the principal was female. The library trustees, her mother's doctor and the few teenaged boys she'd occasionally met through Miss Ivy's club were the only males she really knew. She often found herself watching men like birders watched finches, studying their behavior and trying to make sense of them. She was always startled to discover they were quite human. The ones that were able to be tender with a child were especially fascinating to her. They made her wonder what it would be like to be close enough to truly understand one.

Not that she expected to get close to this one!

She had worked out that he was Zafir, Amineh's brother. Amineh's husband, Ra'id, *hupped* at his camel so it would drop to its knees. He dismounted and the men clasped hands and bent their heads together as they embraced with easy warmth.

Definitely *not* a camel keeper, Fern chided herself. Her students' Uncle Zafir was formally known as Sheikh abu Tariq Zafir ibn Ahmad al-Rakin Iram. He was leader of Q'Amara, the country bordering Ra'id's.

She must have sensed who he was and his stature impacted her, she reasoned. That's why she was suffering this flare of heightened interest. The significance of arriving and meeting such an important man was turning her inside out in a way that was both familiar yet amplified. She was not only shy by nature, but also a redhead with the overactive blushing response that often came with it. She had flushed uncontrollably the first time Ra'id had spoken to her—she'd been so self-conscious under the attention of such a strong personality. A domineering, angry mother had made her sensitive to all authority figures. Anxious to please. It was completely understandable that she'd have an attack of nerves when faced with meeting another sheikh.

She'd never felt blistered from the inside like this, though. Never electrified yet stimulated. It was very disconcerting.

Other men came forward. These ones were camel keepers and camp attendants, but she was aware of only one man now. Not that he noticed her, which was a relief. And why would he? She was buried under a niqab and sunglasses, well-protected against the harsh glare of the sun and the bite of blowing sand. He was busy carrying on two separate conversations with his nieces as they occupied each of his arms.

The girls wriggled to the ground when a boy arrived, crying the name Fern had heard several times since this caravan into the desert had been proposed. "Tariq!"

Their cousin, ten years old, she'd been informed with great awe by her much younger students, wore a long tunic like his father's and challenged the girls to race him up the path to the colorful tents being erected upstream, offering them a head start.

Ra'id helped his wife once her camel was down. Amineh threw off her niqab to hug her brother with all the affection she radiated when talking about him. They all spoke in Arabic, a beautiful language Fern wasn't even close to mastering—

"Oh!" Fern cried as her camel pitched forward.

Remember to lean back, Amineh had cautioned her a million times, but Fern had been so caught up in watching Zafir smile at his sister she hadn't noticed her camel was dropping to its knees. She scrambled to hang on, but was already sliding off by the time the animal hit the ground with a jarring thump.

Her dismount became the clumsiest in Arab history. She barely caught herself from crumpling into a heap. It was witnessed by everyone. So mortifying.

"Are you all right, Fern?" Amineh called. "You seemed to have the trick of it at the last stop. I should have asked Ra'id to help you."

"I'm fine. Just distracted. It's so pretty here," she babbled, trying to cover up her interest in Zafir. A giant magnifying glass might as well be narrowing its beam on her, she was in such a searing, uncomfortable spotlight. She overheard Ra'id say something in Arabic that she did understand, calling her "The English teacher."

"She is," Amineh confirmed. "Come over and meet Fern. Oh, thank you, Nudara," she added as her maid came forward with a canvas bag. Amineh peeled off her abaya and threw it into the bag then motioned for Fern to discard her dusty robe into it as well. "She'll shake the sand out of them so they're ready when the nomads arrive."

Before taking this job, the closest Fern had come to having servants was watching the *Downton Abbey* collection on her laptop. All her life, her mother had been too tired from cleaning other people's houses to do much of it at home, but she'd liked things shipshape. Fern had kept their small flat neat as a pin. In the final months, Fern had provided all-out hospice care, doing everything from bathing her mother to mounting the assistance bar next to the toilet. She still hadn't adjusted to leaving tasks like laundry and cooking to others. It felt presumptuous, even though Nudara took no offense.

Maybe if Fern had been on Amineh's level, making requests of servants wouldn't have bothered her, but she was in that strange limbo between being a servant and being one of the family.

Honestly, she thought with a wry, inward sigh, when had she not been the odd duck set apart from the rest of the group?

This moment was no better. Despite only having adopted the head coverings since taking her position as English tutor to Bashira and Jumanah, Fern felt terribly bold as she removed her dark glasses, unpinned her veil and tugged away both scarf and under cap in one go. It was the hair. Her abundant corkscrews of carrot-orange made everyone in this country do a double take.

She kept her hair long because it was that or resemble a pot scrubber. It probably looked like it had been run through the food processor as it was. She'd been two days without more than a damp facecloth for a bath, but the enormous relief of cool air hitting her sweat-dampened scalp made her prickle with delight. Stripping her abaya, she revealed her sleeveless shirt with its forget-me-not print and lace collar then shook her cornflower-blue skirt from clinging to her legs, self-conscious that it only went to her shins.

"Is this too racy?" she asked Amineh in an undertone. "I didn't know we'd be taking off our abayas in the open like this."

"No, it's fine here," Amineh assured her absently as she stepped away to speak to a servant.

Fern looked to the sheikh for confirmation.

His aqua gaze was traveling over her like tropical seawater, leaving tickling trails down her limbs and making her toes curl in reaction.

Men never looked at her for longer than it took to ask the time or directions. People in general failed to notice her. She dressed conservatively and was fairly plain, didn't wear makeup and spoke softly. Skinny, freckled ginger-haired girls were as common as milk in the village she'd grown up in near the Scottish border.

In this part of the world she stood out, though. Few of the servants back at Ra'id's palace were white and no one was as white as she was. Not that she ran around showing off her arms and legs there. No, the wearing of coverings worked for her. She liked being invisible.

Fat chance right now, though. The sheikh seemed to see through the damp cotton adhered to her skin, cataloguing her every flaw and projecting what she sensed was disapproval. Her heart sank. She hated making missteps, hated being judged and hated it even more when not given a chance to prove herself first.

"Welcome to the oasis," he said.

His husky baritone wafted over her like a hot breeze, spreading a ripple of disconcerting awareness through her. Similar to Amineh's English, his accent held an intriguing mix of exotic Middle East and cool, upper-class Brit. Zafir was all man.

A widower, according to Amineh. His wife had died of cancer three years ago. *It hit him hard. He doesn't talk about her much. When he does, it's always with great admiration*, Amineh had said.

That meant she ought to be feeling sympathy toward him, Fern thought, but experienced a rush of defensive animosity. She didn't like it. For the most part, she avoided conflict of any kind. If she was cornered, she was perfectly capable of lashing out with vicious sarcasm, but she hated being that person so she tried not to let it happen.

But he was looking at her as though he knew something about her. Like whatever assumption he reached made him cynical and dismayed.

His continued study made her hyperaware of herself. Reflexively, she started doing Miss Ivy's bolstering exercises, reminding herself of all her good qualities. She was smart and kind, good at crafts if she had a pattern to follow...

Distantly, she realized this was a hugely protective reaction. He was a stranger and Miss Ivy always urged patience and not leaping to conclusions about what a new acquaintance might think.

But along with an irrational, panicked certainty that he had taken an instant dislike to her, she *felt* his rebuff in a way that was surprisingly devastating. She wasn't a snob, not even an intellectual one, didn't put on airs despite knowing the Dewey decimal system inside and out… Why on earth would she feel a near irresistible urge to tell him that? She wasn't here to impress him and *wouldn't* with statements like that.

But she was intimidated by the kind of man he was. So imperious. When had she ever come into the sphere of anyone like him? The natural instincts of the weak wanted someone this powerful to be on her side. She recognized that, but there was something else going on inside her, something she'd never really experienced before. She feared it might be attraction. Not a passing "oh, he's nice-looking," but something far more elemental. *Please consider me.*

That involuntary yearning was deeply confusing and beyond inappropriate.

A blush began to climb from her tight chest into her closing throat and across her face until her ears felt like they were on fire. She hated herself then. Hated her body and its over-the-top reaction. She was embarrassed by her own embarrassment and wanted to die.

* * *

Zafir watched a million freckles disappear in a bath of red and felt an unexpected urge to laugh.

Not nice, he realized, glancing away to hide the amusement brimming his eyes. He didn't want to soften toward this English teacher, who was drowning in her own blush of sexual attraction. He was experienced enough to know that's what was happening to her and man enough to like it.

But *English*.

Despite knowing how inappropriate she was for him, the prowling tomcat within him kept his tail standing at attention. His eyes traveled back to her of their own accord, counting the freckles that dotted her arms like cocoa sprinkled onto foamed milk. They were all over her, even the tops of her feet. The full effect naked would be an incredible sight.

One he would not make any attempts to see, he cautioned his libido, no matter how amenable she might seem.

He lifted his gaze from her disaster of a skirt, to shoulders covered in that Milky Way of freckles barely visible against the pink of her extensive blush, to liquid eyes locked on his face. He recognized the look, which was somewhere between nervous bunny and dazzled groupie.

Being a duke's grandson had entitled him to more than an academic education. Alongside economics and diplomacy, he'd learned that Western women could be incredibly accommodating to a man's basest needs. If he wanted her, he could have her.

That's why he began fantasizing about setting his mouth against her shoulder, feeling the heat under her skin and tasting that smooth, pale flesh. That's why his palm tingled to push into the folds of her skirt, to discover the shape of her backside and lock her hips into his own.

But tanned blondes were his preference. American or Scandinavian and only while traveling. He had enough power struggles with the conservatives in his country without having affairs inside his borders. He dismissed her with an arrogant blink, deliberately letting her see his rejection.

She swallowed, face blazing and lashes dropping. The corners of her lips pulled into the tortured bite of her teeth.

He had a near irresistible urge to cover her pursed doll's mouth with his own, to lightly torture her until her lips were swollen and open. He could practically feel that wild hair tangled around his fingers as he held her under him, her clasp on him tight as he thrust deep and watched her eyes fog with ecstasy.

English, he reminded with a mild curse at his own weakness. Was it genetic that he could be blindsided by lust for one, so much so that he couldn't smile, let alone speak?

He was only responding to her because he hadn't been with any woman in over two months, he reasoned. It had nothing to do with a tainted streak in his makeup. He wasn't like his father, who had fallen so hard for the wrong woman he'd gotten himself killed for it, leaving his bastard half-blood son to clean up the mess.

"Fern, this is my brother, Zafir. She may call you that while we're here, yes?" Amineh turned back and clasped his arm, then leaned her weight on him in a familiar way that yanked him back into awareness. "Be nice to her. She's shy."

Fern. It was oddly suitable. His country favored names inspired by nature and something in her buttoned-down demeanor reminded him of those tightly curled fiddleheads he used to spy when tramping through his grandfather's estate, searching for signs of spring and the end of the semester, when he could return to the warmth of home.

"Of course," he managed to respond, fine with the level of stiffness in his tone. He was in the throes of a very wrong-time, wrong-place reaction. The feeling annoyed him enough to reflect in his voice. Still, he heard himself say, "If I may call you Fern." He would regardless, but he willed permission from her all the same. Cooperation.

Capitulation.

Damn. He really shouldn't want her so badly that he was already finding ways to stake a claim. Like it was a given that he would have her. This was lust. Garden-variety. He was on vacation, relaxed. Horny. Of course he responded to an available woman. That's all this was and he could resist it.

Her lashes quivered and she nodded shakily, fingers playing together restlessly.

Her discomfiture left him grimly pleased. He was vital and sexual and alpha. Asserting himself was second nature, but there was more at play here. Amineh might see only a blush, but Fern's reaction was carnal and that held a special allure for him.

"We're very informal here," Amineh chattered on. "We'll cover up again when the Bedouins come through, but for now the oasis is ours. That's why I love it. Oh, I've been looking forward to this." She squeezed his arm again, then gave him a frown. "But you look grumpy. Why? We're going to have fun. Act like kids again. Come on, Fern. Let's walk up to the camp and get settled."

Fern began to gather her bags onto her shoulder.

Zafir bit back an urging for her to leave them for the servants, but she was Ra'id's employee, he reminded himself. Not an ambassador's daughter. She knew her place better than he did.

She packed like an ambassador's daughter, he noted with a grimace, as he watched her try to heft a third bag onto her shoulder.

He moved to take it.

"I can come back for it," she insisted, but he brushed past her attempts to keep it and reached to remove one of the others already bending her slender spine. His thumb grazed skin like duck down, punching a shot of hot need into his gut.

What the hell? From barely touching her?

The hair on his scalp stood on end with both alarm and excitement.

She dipped her head, making it impossible for him to decipher whether she had reacted as intensely. But if he wasn't mistaken, her nipples were standing up in sharp points. It couldn't be from a chill in this heat.

Which should not make his belly tighten with anticipation, but it did.

Amineh was halfway up the path with Ra'id, leaving him to accompany Fern. He forced himself to find a neutral topic of conversation.

"The oasis is roughly seventeen square kilometers. My father designated this as a nature reserve when we were children. We have one tribe allowed to camp here without a permit as they follow bird migrations. We anticipate they'll come through while we're here, but otherwise access is strictly limited."

"I read about it before we came." Her quick statement seemed to say "thanks, but I know all I need to." She hurried along.

Let it go, he told himself. Let *her* go. If she had received the message that he wasn't welcome to a come-on, that was a good thing.

But his longer legs easily kept up to the scurrying pace that kept the color high in her cheeks. And he couldn't take his eyes off the way her remarkable hair bounced and her small, firm breasts barely moved.

And all the while, she looked straight ahead as though trying to ignore him.

"How long have you been teaching the girls?" he asked.

"Three months." She flashed a look up at him that was vaguely defensive. "I feel a bit of a fraud, to be honest. Amineh, I mean, umm, Bashira…"

"It's fine," he said. "As she said, we're casual here. No need to use her title."

"Right. Thank you. What I was going to say is that her English is perfect and the girls are already switching back and forth very easily. Aside from correcting their grammar and spelling, I'm not sure they really need me. It's just such a remarkable opportunity to experience another culture and…" She cleared her throat and her gaze flickered over him like a searchlight picking out the best parts. "The girls are lovely," she murmured faintly. "I feel very fortunate to be here. Well, there. *And* here."

Another blush. She was really in the throes of sexual interest. How utterly captivating. The hormones that told a man to pursue a woman seared his veins like adrenaline.

"I'm sure she's delighted to have you in the household," he said, his voice as tight as his skin, brain somehow maintaining a grasp on the conversation. "My sister and I prefer our father's world, but we often feel homesick for England." He closed his mouth, not sure why he had said it like that. It wasn't real homesickness, just that all his life he'd wished he could live in both places at the same time.

Which felt like a traitorous admission, as though he wasn't wholly committed to the country he ruled, but he was. Willing to make deep sacrifices for it even. He frowned.

Beside him, Fern halted abruptly and cast a jerky glance up and down the beach. It was a scene of controlled chaos: tents going up, pillows spilling from baskets and silk rugs unrolled. "I, um, don't know where I'm going. Do I sleep with the children?"

"No, they have their own tent." He pointed to where his son was hanging the partition between his side and the girls' in the undersized tent they used.

The servants were settling near the water pump at the far end of the beach, where the cooking fire would be laid. A large tent was going up not far from the children's, for Amineh and Ra'id. His own tent was already standing at the end of a small bench of sand facing the water. Security would place their small tents at strategic places at the perimeter of the oasis.

Deductive reasoning allowed him to single out the only unclaimed lodging. Halfway between the two ends of the camp, tucked beneath an overhang of palms where a small footprint of sand pushed into the tall grass, sat a bundled tent.

Apparently Fern was expected to know how to erect the tent herself.

"That one," he said, as he grazed light fingers on her upper arm to catch her attention then pointed.

Yes, he was that weak. Unable to resist touching her.

Her breath caught and he experienced a surprisingly strong pulse of satisfaction that she responded so sharply to his barely there caress.

This was going to be a difficult two weeks.

Fern wished Zafir would take a hike so she could figure out what was going on.

Obviously she found him attractive. Who wouldn't? He was gorgeous. And he'd noticed, *obviously*, because she was useless at disguising her thoughts and feelings. That's why she preferred to hide behind books and library desks and had taken a job a million miles from home so she'd only have two students and hardly see any men at all.

Men made her nervous. Not outright afraid. They'd have to notice her for her to feel threatened, but she'd learned the hardest way possible not to beg for approval. As much as she might have a curiosity about dating and mating, she was highly reluctant to put her hard-won confidence on the line. It had been far easier over the years to stay home and *not* rile her mother by going out with men. Instead, she had excelled at her studies and worked hard to help pay rent and, yes, had even taken a martyr's pride in being the dutiful daughter. She'd told herself she was too busy for romance, but really, she'd been too cowardly.

Or perhaps, hadn't met a man exciting enough to provoke her past her reservations. The fact that something had been awakened in her today, made her want to be noticed and appreciated and found worthy, made her anxious. Emotionally vulnerable.

And disturbingly aware of herself physically. She'd never responded to a man in such an animal way. Her knowledge about sex was mostly gleaned from the deliciously graphic passages in romance novels. They always gave her a nice flush of pleasure, but thinking about doing those sorts of things in real life, wondering what Zafir liked to do to women and what it might feel like to have his hands and mouth on her naked body, made sharp sensations pierce her nipples and between her thighs. Heat that was both embarrassment and excitement throbbed painfully in her, making her feel all the more defenseless and exposed.

It was *so* unnerving.

This was why her mother had always said sex was dangerous. Fern had wondered why so many people did it if it was so bad, but until today she'd never had a man touch her. Not really. Not so she felt it like a lightning bolt into her belly. *That* was why people did it. The sensations were compelling enough to overcome logic and common sense.

She desperately wanted to move away from him and take time to examine exactly what was happening to her, label it, then put it in storage forever. Especially because some primal part of her felt like he... But no. She was making it up. Fretting because that's what she did best. She was misinterpreting basic courtesy as...

She didn't even know the words for what she

thought she sensed, only that she felt like she was trapped in a tiger's cage and he was pacing around her, curious enough to sniff, but not genuinely hungry. Bored maybe. Looking for something to play with.

He walked across to drop her bags by a red bundle.

Oh, dear. Was that her tent? Well, she wasn't above reading directions. She tried to retrieve the card from its plastic pocket.

"I'll do it," he said, looking disgruntled as he picked up the bundle, opened the drawstring and shook the contents onto the sand. He discarded the nylon outer bag.

"I'm sure I can work it out." She picked up the empty bag and turned it over to see the card was covered in foreign cursive.

"Do you read Arabic?" he asked dryly, then handed her a corner of the tent and backed away to shake out the large square.

"Not yet," she answered, moving to extend the other corner. As she did, she picked up the bag of pegs so they wouldn't be caught underneath. "Is there really no English? Because this doesn't look like traditional Bedouin accommodation."

"No, these modern designs are too lightweight and practical to ignore for the sake of custom." He snagged the small mallet she drew from the bag of pegs. "Even the nomads have moved to lighter fabrics than woven camel hair, but you'll see more authentic tents when they come through." He held out his hand for a peg.

"I can manage. I'll ask one of the other men if I can't. I don't want to inconvenience you." There. She had an assertive side. It was very polite and obliging, but it got the job done when she needed it.

He flicked his sharp gaze around the camp as though looking for one of these men she might enlist when really, she'd probably ask Amineh's maid for help before she'd find the courage to approach a stranger and beg a favor.

When his gaze came back to hers, he seemed disapproving and vaguely challenging. "I'll do it," he stated.

She locked her teeth, having learned long ago to pick her battles.

At least she was able to hurry the process. She willed her fingers to be nimble as she followed him down the side and across the back of the tent, struggling all the loops onto the pegs as he hammered them into the sand. The feeling of having her every action scrutinized was her own baggage, she reminded herself as she moved toward the front. He wasn't watching her. He was having some kind of manly back-to-nature moment, indulging his instinct to prove his superiority over nature.

Nevertheless, as she straightened from making the last attachment, the tension was killing her. She glanced at him and his green eyes were waiting, snagging her like a hook, with a pierce and a tug.

She caught her breath, limbs paralyzed with shock.

He calmly continued what he was doing, and lengthened a pole in increments with a smooth stroke of his hand and a light twist of his wrist, eyes staying on her like they'd been there a while.

He lifted the opening of the tent and slid the pole inside.

It was…

She blushed. God help her, she blushed hard.

A noise escaped him. Might have been a snort of amusement or a *tsk* of impatience. She wasn't sure because he bent to take up another shortened pole and began to extend it. When his gaze came back to hers, his was fierce and almost scolding.

His rebuke burned. She knew her reaction was obvious. Her ability to demure was nil. Worse, she knew she didn't inspire male desire. She wasn't particularly curvy on her chest or bottom. She wouldn't know how to apply eye shadow if she'd ever had the spare notes to buy it. Between the braces to fix terribly crooked teeth, the second-hand clothes, the extra studies to win a scholarship and then maintaining her position at the library while she earned her degree, she'd been the most easily overlooked nerd her entire life.

Maybe he was one of those jocks who occasionally noticed she was an easy mark and was having his fun teasing her. Maybe he was silently taunting her, sending a pithy "as if."

She usually walked away when feeling picked on, but despite the seventeen square kilometers around her, she didn't have anywhere to go. The only place she could hide from Zafir was her own quarters, so she ducked into them. She bendt under the light weight of the silky red fabric to pick up the pole from the ground and worked her way to the center, where a grommet awaited on the roof and the floor.

Of course it wasn't as easy as it looked. She got the top one hooked in, but even though the tent wasn't heavy, the tension in the fabric was resistant to her attempts to align the bottom of the pole into the floor.

"You spaced the pegs too far away," she told him, hearing her mother's voice and cringing.

"I've pitched more tents than you have, Fern," he drawled and she narrowed her eyes at him even though they couldn't see each other.

Another pole made a zipping noise as he slid it into the pocket that would form one of the corners. "Let me finish this part then I'll help you."

Oh, great. I'll just stand here looking stupid then.

The tent shifted on her hair, making it crackle with static. She debated crawling out, but couldn't make herself go out there and face him.

Another *zip, zip, zip* and he had the back and walls stabilized.

Leave when he comes in, she thought, but he lifted the front of the tent and took up all the space, bringing the middle of the tent pole so it slid through her light grip and the roof climbed as he neared her. Then he was standing before her, the narrow pole between them, his tanned face tinged by the translucent red of the fabric, his gaze fixed on hers.

He slid his hands over her limp ones and guided the bottom end of the pole into place.

She tried to look away, but he was tall and very close. He smelled good. Earthy and sweaty, but not overpowering. Masculine and intriguing. Aside from her mother's specialist, she'd never met a man with such an air of command and that physician had been white-haired and potbellied. Zafir was in his prime, not just healthy, but radiating supremacy.

In the back of her mind, she knew she was behaving like some kind of rock-band superfan, speechless in the presence of a man with star quality, unable to move, but he was so incredible. She found herself staring into his eyes for too long. She knew it was too long, but she couldn't look away from those crystal blue-green depths. They quested, delving into hers, demanding something she didn't even understand.

Say something, she thought, and let her tongue wet her lips.

His gaze lowered to her mouth.

Her breath evaporated.

She found her own gaze dropping to his mouth, wondering how it would feel to have those smooth lips rubbing against hers. Her heart was fluttering like a trapped bird, her pulse pounding in her ears.

He lifted his hand to hover hotly next to her cheek, scorching her. His brows jerked in some type of struggle. *Was he going to kiss her?*

It was remarkable yet terrifying. Did she really want to do this? It was so wrong, but he was *right there*.

"Miss Davenport, are you in there?" Bashira called from outside.

Fern's heart went into free fall. Her conscience gave her a hard shake and she jerked back, shocked.

"I am," she stammered, discovering her hand was still trapped under Zafir's on the pole.

His grip tightened briefly before he released her with a flare of his fingers. He lifted away his touch as though she'd burned him. A muscle ticked in his cheek. He looked very displeased. Accusatory, but also confused.

She surreptitiously touched her mouth, and avoided looking at him as she edged around him to open the flap of the tent.

The rush of fresh air, dry and hot as it was, made her realize how stifling it had been inside, where things had been sultry and musky. Her heart was still pounding hard and loud. It took everything she had to muster a smile for the children as they approached.

"Mama said these are for you." Bashira struggled with Jumanah to drag a basket across the sand toward her. Tariq followed, staggering under the weight of a bedroll on his shoulder.

"Have you met my son?" Zafir asked as he emerged beside her. He didn't stand so close as to be improper, but the air crackled with energy that bounced back and forth between them.

Fern stepped forward to escape the field of it. "Not yet."

What had just happened in there? Was he messing with her? She hadn't known what to expect from Amineh's brother, but cruelty wasn't on the list. The thought that he would toy with her for his own amusement was not only painful, but also opened the gap of deep vulnerability in her even wider. She wouldn't be able to avoid him here.

He moved forward to take the bedroll off his son, introduced the boy then disappeared inside the tent to lay it out.

Far too intimate a thing to do. How was she supposed to sleep on something he had touched?

"Your cousins speak very highly of you, Tariq," she said shakily. "I'm looking forward to getting to know you."

The boy regarded her with a very serious expression. Not his father's eyes, thank goodness. His were like black coffee, but they held the same intelligence and confidence.

"They speak well of you, too, but may I say with all proper respect that I no longer have need of a nanny. I have a guard." He quarter turned to indicate a man observing from a position near the children's tent. "To protect me from outside threats. I am allowed to make my own mistakes and learn from them."

Pleasantly diverted by that statement, Fern nodded. "I can see you're mature enough to do so. But I'm not a nanny. I tutor the girls in English."

"I'm on vacation," Tariq stated promptly. "My English is excellent."

Abundant self-assurance was obviously a genetic trait. Her lips were still fiery and buzzing from having Zafir stare at them. Now they twitched with amusement.

"I hope you'll join us for our field lessons anyway," Fern said. "I'm excited to explore the oasis. I brought a microscope, some tracking books and sketching supplies. Perhaps you could teach me some things about your country and its wildlife."

"Oh, yes, I could do that," he stated with generosity. "My father is also very knowledgeable," he said as Zafir emerged again to stand at her side. "He finds an animal even when it's trying to hide."

Fern outright refused to look at Zafir with that remark hovering like a balloon ready to burst. She was not interested in being laughed at even more.

"That would be a treat," she murmured, throat tightening with indignation. "But he's already gone out of his way on my behalf. I don't want to impose."

"You would do it for my cousins, wouldn't you, Baba?" Tariq said, neck craned to look up at his father.

"Of course," Zafir promised with a hand clasping warmly to Tariq's shoulder. "That's why we are here. To spend time with our family. You'll show our guest where to find everything? I can't put off confirming that everyone has arrived safely as scheduled." Turning to her, Zafir explained, "Rescues are difficult and time sensitive, so we have very low criteria for setting them off. Any delay of a message will do it. Excuse me."

As if nothing had happened between them, he nodded and walked away.

Of course, nothing *had* happened, she reminded herself. Maybe she'd imagined that whole thing.

Except her cheek still burned where he'd almost touched her.

She forced her gaze not to linger on his back, but she couldn't help wondering what that back would look like naked. Tanned and strong. When had she ever, ever fantasized about running light fingers down a man's spine? Or sprawling naked upon one?

This place was supernatural, casting a spell of some kind over her.

Distressed, she forced her attention to the children. They showed her where to find boiled water for drinking and pointed out the latrine and gave her a short broom to use to sweep out scorpions— really?—if they wandered into her tent. Then they left her to unpack as they scampered off in search of wild dates.

Fern entered the privacy of her tent and let out a long, anxious breath. Amineh had talked about the oasis like it was a place of freedom, but Fern had a sense of being kidnapped—into luxury, sure. The tent was bigger than the tiny bedroom she'd grown up in. The bedding and pillows the children had brought her were silky and colorful, while the pallet Zafir had unrolled was wide enough for two.

Stop it.

How had she even wound up here at the end of the earth? She'd grown up expecting she would take a position in a village day school, perhaps going home to a tidy flat where she'd have a cat named Fabio. Her only aspiration had been to provide the same ray of hope Miss Ivy had instilled in her—to help withdrawn, unhappy students discover their own hidden potential.

Hers had apparently been the ability to become an international teacher.

She hadn't even considered an overseas position while her mother had been alive, but after her mother had passed away, Fern had needed a fresh start. On a whim, she'd applied to a placement agency and expected to wind up in a missionary school, but had found herself in the running for this job.

It still felt like a miracle that she'd won it, but her quiet nature seemed to fit with a culture that valued modesty. She and Amineh had got on immediately, which surprised Fern. At first she had thought it was only because Amineh appreciated Fern's genuine affection for the girls and her earnest desire to act in their best interests. Now she knew Amineh better, she recognized a like soul in the sense that they'd both struggled to find their place in the jungle of female cliques during their school years.

Amineh and Zafir, Fern had learned, were the product of a rather notorious affair between an Arab sheikh and an English duke's daughter. They'd ping-ponged back and forth between their parents, not quite fitting fully into either culture. Amineh had found stability by marrying her brother's best friend, Ra'id, and living permanently in his country.

Zafir still fought for the right to rule their father's homeland, Q'Amara. He'd married the daughter of a sheikh, trying to ease resistance at having a man with such heavy Western influences governing their country.

Somehow she couldn't picture him wearing the same sad frown Amineh wore when she talked about their difficult early years. He seemed too fiercely proud to allow prejudice to reach his heart. It was hard to imagine a man that dynamic and confident struggling with anything.

Peeking out of her tent, she saw him down at the water, shin-deep in the spring where the children had told her bathing was allowed. He stood with his sharp profile angled upward to the top of the worn canyon on the far side of the water. Then he crouched, not taking any heed that his robe was soaked through. He scooped his hands into the water and splashed his face, then lifted his *gutra* to wet the back of his neck.

She swallowed, going weak as she watched him. He was so comfortable in his skin, so self-assured and compelling.

It dawned on her that this was a crush. She was suffering a full-blown case of unfounded infatuation, behaving exactly like her adolescent schoolmates used to. She stood here spying on a boy, acting geeky and awkward and keyed up, entertaining uncharacteristic fantasies of kissing the back of his neck. How puerile. If only his wife was alive to deter her.

Look away, she told herself, but she couldn't make herself do it. Why did he have to be out there acting all brooding and sexy anyway?

He stood and turned to stare directly at her tent. His shoulders were set at what seemed a tense angle, his demeanor projecting dissatisfaction.

She couldn't tell if he saw her, but she retreated to the back wall.

This was going to be an interminable two weeks.

CHAPTER TWO

FERN USED THE excuse of ferreting out her supplies and setting up her mock classroom to avoid everyone for the rest of the day. She usually ate alone so when she smelled the evening meal, she found Nudara, who fetched her a bowl of spicy stew and flatbread with some kind of yogurt dolloped on top.

Taking it back to her tent, Fern told herself the peacefulness was nice. The bustle of the camp settled as everyone sat to eat. The children's laughter rang out often, along with Amineh's and the occasional rich male chuckle—one of which made Fern listen harder and feel…

She sighed and shook her head at herself. The light breeze whispered through the palm leaves above her, snickering. An unknown bird tittered at her.

It grew dark quickly, but the nearly full moon rose shortly after. The trip had been organized around the fattest moon as that was the likeliest time for the Bedouins to visit the oasis. The waxing orb's glow turned the landscape a pale blue and a velvety breeze caressed her cheek as she walked her dishes back to the outdoor kitchen.

Later, after she had brushed her teeth, she put herself to bed early. She'd had a long, active couple of days, she told herself, even though she could hear the children laughing over music from a stringed instrument. No one else was turning in yet. They were visiting and having fun.

Sociology classes had taught her this sort of camp built the relationships between members of a tribe. The servants were certainly in good spirits, teasing one another and making jokes. Zafir's coming together with his neighbor, Ra'id, had strengthened relations between their two countries in ancient ways, even if they only traded gossip. Corporations called something like this a "team-building exercise" and paid small fortunes for their employees to attend.

Fern was the luckiest person in the world to be able to experience this.

She told herself.

As she held her eyes closed against an inexplicable sting.

She had absolutely no reason to feel lonely in this wide bed. Miss Ivy would enjoy hearing about all of this when Fern had an online connection again.

Make some notes, she cajoled herself, but didn't move. Instead she mentally wrote something entirely different, something that belonged in an erotic novel. It was a scene where Zafir came to her tent and touched a lot more than her cheek.

It was the worst night of her life. She tossed and turned, unable to shut off her mind from conjuring fantasies of making love with Zafir.

She didn't even know how it was properly done! Obviously she knew the mechanics, but she'd been firmly sheltered from any sort of expressions of sexual passion. Her mother hadn't allowed her to go to sexy movies or watch any of those daytime serials on television. The romance novels at the library had been read from an angle under the desk. Guilt always assailed her for enjoying those stories and more than one academic friend had shamed her for picking them up, but Fern couldn't help wondering why was it so bad to like stories about love and happily-ever-after?

Because of the sex, her mother's voice said in her head. Heaven help any woman who gave in to her hormones. That only brought heartache and disappointment.

Fern being the disappointment in question, she had long ago surmised.

Yet here she was, indulging her own hormones with imaginary banquets of kisses and caresses.

It wasn't the first time she'd lain in bed and imagined she wasn't alone, but she'd never been quite so explicit with her fantasies or had a particular man in mind.

It had to stop.

Throwing off her light sheet, she quietly unzipped her tent and stepped into the cool of predawn. The camp was silent, the stillness only broken by the relentless pounding of her pulse.

Dressed in her knee-length cotton nightgown, she walked down to the beach and sighed as her feet found the damp sand at the water's edge. The burning inside her began to ease. This was what she'd needed. A cold shower.

Was that why Zafir had come to the water yesterday?

No. No more daydreams that he fancied her. He'd only been washing off travel grime.

Still, she found herself tracking to the place where he'd stood in the water. It felt deliciously cool as it closed over her feet and climbed to the backs of her knees.

Drawn forward, she sucked in a breath as the pool deepened quickly, soaking through to weigh the fabric of her nightgown. Chilly water hit her loins, then her navel. She sucked in her stomach, got as far as her breasts and held her breath.

She dipped until the cold water closed over her and stayed under a moment, nose plugged, letting the chill seep to her bones. Then she titled back her head and rose, baptized into a creature of this foreign yet intoxicating world.

The thought made her smile naturally for the first time since arriving here. Oh, she felt a million times better!

Which was silly. One little plunge into a spring couldn't wash away a lifetime of baggage and misgivings, but she wished it could be that easy. Her mother's shaking finger always seemed to follow her, though, undermining her ability to enjoy the simplest sensual experience. She would no doubt criticize her for... Well, everything. Her mother wouldn't approve of anything Fern had done since the service. Ever in her life, really.

At least she wasn't burning with desire for a man beyond her reach anymore. She thought she could sleep now and escape all her disturbing ruminations about Zafir.

Turning, she marveled at how clear the water was, completely entranced by its perfection, feeling mammalian and part of the universe as she watched her feet. Not all creatures were herd animals, she reminded herself. Many lived alone most of their lives, only seeking another of their kind to mate—

Bare, tanned feet stood on the beach before her. Her heart stalled and her soggy nightgown clung like a skin of dread. Her feet halted and her knees locked in denial.

How? No one else was up.

Her gaze climbed athletic shins to where unbleached linen board shorts ended at his knees.

Leave it to him to wear drawstring shorts that were still the epitome of class, tailored to hang low across his brown hips in the most disreputable yet erotic way. He wasn't wearing a shirt and he was a perfect specimen of the human male. His tense, flat abs were bisected by a line of hair that flared across his brown chest. The pattern accentuated his broad shoulders and the relaxed muscles of his upper arms.

His mouth was set in a grim line, the stubble on his jaw dark making him look even more piratical and dangerous than the first glimpse she'd had of him. He had black hair, she noted. Trimmed close to keep it tight against his scalp.

His brows stayed heavy over those remarkable, glittering eyes as he opened a towel with a flick. She hadn't noticed he was holding one. He beckoned her with two bent fingers, then hissed a word in Arabic that she'd heard Amineh use to hurry the girls.

"Now," he said in a stern whisper. "The guards don't need to see you like that."

Like what?

She glanced down to see her nightgown was

plastered to her front, her nipples standing out from the high curves of her breasts like traffic cones. Her lack of underwear was flagrantly obvious.

The light was coming up fast with the sun. She couldn't approach him looking like this!

Her tent looked miles away from here, however, and… *Oh, help me*. He didn't wait. He waded into the water and snapped the towel around her back, barely giving her a chance to lift her arms out of the way before he closed it across her chest and tucked it tight.

She grabbed at it to finish the job herself, then brushed his hands away and glared up at him, even though she was the idiot who'd gotten herself into this mortifying position.

"I didn't think anyone else was awake," she hissed.

"The guards patrol around the clock."

She scowled at the surrounding area, right up to the top of the jagged wall of the canyon, seeing no one. "Well, I wasn't planning to swim when I came out."

"Good thing I was." He nodded at the towel, matching her whisper, but still managing to sound patronizing.

"I wasn't trying to insult anyone," she explained, upset that she'd made a cultural gaffe.

He snorted. "That was the least of my reasons for covering you."

Again he used the tone that suggested she was a bit of a half-wit. She glared up at him, but the eye contact only sent a current of electricity through her that stayed active and hummed in her veins so her breaths stumbled unevenly. A shiver chased over her even as the burn that had kept her awake through the night rekindled.

She forced herself to look toward her tent. Told her feet to carry her in that direction, but all the illicit fantasies she'd had in there loomed large in her mind. The blood she'd cooled with her swim heated and moved with a sensual slither through her veins, creating a simmering warmth in her belly and lower. Very personal muscles clenched in anticipation.

The return to a state of receptiveness was so primeval and quick, her breath hitched in a helpless catch. How did he do this to her by only standing near? It was unsettling to have no control over her reactions.

She didn't want to know if he knew, hoped he didn't, but her gaze tracked to his to see.

He was waiting for her. Something fierce flashed in his eyes. This time when he stepped close and lowered his head, as proprietary as a man could get, she didn't feel any alarm. No sense of self-preservation. Just anticipation. *Please*.

His lips burned on contact against her cool

ones, sliding easily against the dampness left from her swim.

Her eyes closed and her senses came alive to the feel of his firm mouth settling purposefully onto hers. He parted her lips with a lick of his tongue, causing heat to flow into them so fast it stung. Her whole body came alive with a jolt of powerful excitement so intense she shuddered.

And she returned the pressure of his mouth instinctively, moving hers in a type of hungry greed, Her heart pounded with excitement and fear-spiked awareness that she wanted things from him he could never give her. This was futile, but irresistible.

And so exquisite. When his tongue dashed deeper against her inner lips, both daring and deliciously stimulating, she touched her own to his. He tasted smoky and spicy, not like cigarettes, but like open fires and exotic foods. He was remarkable. The sensations he provoked in her were so sweet she wanted to moan aloud. She was drowning—

It hit her that they were still standing in the pool where anyone could see them.

Stricken, she jerked back with a splashing step.

He steadied her, mouth tightening to a harsh line as he scanned over her head. When his searing green gaze came back to hers, his eyes were brimming with frustration.

"Let's take this to my tent," he said in a graveled undertone.

Her heart exploded inside her chest like an overinflated balloon, bursting into ragged pieces. Hookups were just that easy? Women were, she supposed. For him. He obviously thought she was.

"Just like that?" she asked breathily, anguished that she'd dropped herself so low in his estimation.

He cocked his head, expression cynical. "You don't want to?"

His tone was full of the knowledge that she'd kissed him back, making it doubly hard to claim she didn't want to. Her chest was still rising jaggedly and her vision was full of a naked chest she longed to touch. She swallowed.

"I happen to like my job," she said, hating herself for not being able to honestly say she wasn't even tempted. She was. Deeply.

"They don't have to know," he said, flatly brushing that away.

"Look." She must be glowing redder than the sky at the horizon. "I can do the math. You don't have many options here." She used her chin to indicate the camp. "I suppose it's a good offer, that I should feel flattered, but I'm not in your league."

It was a detail she'd been using in her head to counter her longing and it didn't seem to sway him any better than it did her.

His expression hardened with derision. "We'll be on exactly the same level once we're horizontal."

Nice, she mentally scoffed, taking that remark like a sword in the gut, while the thought of being horizontal, with him atop her, shorted out her brain.

She startled at the way his hand gentled on her arm as it moved in a light caress that raised prickling sensations across her shoulders and up the back of her neck. He was making no effort to temper his sexuality and was quite overwhelming. Everything about him made her heart race with both apprehension and excitement. His touch was so possessive and strong that every little caress of his thumb against her skin would stay with her for the rest of her life.

"You really want me to believe you don't want to?" he chided.

"Of course I want to," she admitted painfully. There was no point in denying it. She was lousy at dissembling. Stronger people walked all over her because she had few natural defenses. It made her great with children and hopeless when it came to a captivating man like him.

So she realized what a chance she was taking in revealing how attracted she was to him. If he took it into his head to pursue her, she'd have no way of stopping him.

"Then let it happen." His reassuring caress became something more, something drugging and inducing. "I'm not going to hurt you, Fern."

"I've been given to believe differently," she protested with the caustic sarcasm she hated resorting to, but her back was to the wall. "Apparently it does hurt. The first time."

So there, she told him with a pointed look into stunned aqua eyes. Her face ached. *Yes*, she mentally transmitted. No one had ever wanted her enough to take her virginity. It was lowering and painful, but it was true.

Now her feet found the ability to propel her away to somewhere dark and small. Chest aching, she let her shaky legs carry her back to her tent.

Her plan was to shamelessly use the children as deflective shields if Zafir approached her, but he didn't.

Which was unconscionably disappointing.

But what did she think? That she was irresistible? With this bedhead?

She'd woken from a deep sleep that had been an escape from a desire to cry. If an unfamiliar towel hadn't been lying in a heap next to her still damp nightgown, she might have thought she'd dreamed the whole thing.

Sadly she hadn't. And now Zafir knew she was a virgin. One who was inordinately hot for him.

Funny how Mother was always right. Lust *did* make you miserable. Fern supposed she ought to be glad it hadn't also got her pregnant, kicked out of her home and abandoned by the father. She wouldn't be so busy trying to make ends meet and raising a burden alone that life would pass her by in an astringent blur.

"Excellent!" Tariq declared, making Fern look up from kneeling next to Bashira as she helped the girl focus the microscope.

"What is?" she prompted, but a tickling shiver chased up her spine and she knew without following Tariq's gaze over her head.

"My father is coming to take us for a walk."

Standing, she pivoted to face Zafir, taking a breath to argue, but he stole her ability to speak simply by arriving and casting a respectful eye over her overturned wicker basket and tablet, which showed pictures of water bugs.

The girls leaped up to fetch proper shoes.

"Why…?" she asked, feeling persecuted.

"You're safe, Fern," he assured her, one hand lifting to calm her as he held his distance.

She didn't feel safe! Not when his sweeping gaze seemed to visualize her nude beneath a soaked gown. She crossed her arms, hiding that her nipples prickled into points and trying to protect the fragile ego squirming like a wisp of smoke behind her breastbone.

"I shouldn't have presumed this morning." A mixture of compunction and frustration flashed in his expression. "If I frightened you, I apologize." He sounded sincere. Looked it, even though his gaze was now penetrating hers in a way that was extremely uncomfortable. "It won't happen again."

Well, that certainly told her how irresistible she was. Her eyes grew damp with a startling mixture of frustration and longing. She lowered her lashes to hide her completely misplaced disappointment.

"Lust is bad," she managed to say, stating it for her own benefit, hoping to soothe this sting of rejection by making it sound like she wouldn't go to bed with him even if he wanted her to.

His mouth twitched, the corners deepening with a pained and secretive smile. "Says the woman who doesn't know what she's talking about." He sobered into the man she had read was a determined leader of a troubled populace. "But in this case, yes. The consequences aren't worth it."

A thick lump rose in her throat. His words cut to the bone and set her adrift. Funny how it really didn't matter that Zafir's kiss had been incidental, brought on by proximity and availability, nothing personal. She had done what females did around all alpha males: projected willingness. His reaction had been as biological as hers.

She shouldn't want him to do it again, but she did.

Lust. Hormones. Whatever it was, they were very detrimental to a woman's good sense. She ought to thank him for dismissing any possibility of giving in to it.

But she was just hurt.

He smiled and offered, "I'm only here because Tariq pled your case at lunch."

"*My* case?"

"His own," he answered with a tilt of his head. "Ra'id has asked you not to take the girls beyond the camp without him, but he has agreed with Tariq that I am an acceptable escort."

"I—" *think*, she urged herself "—don't want to impose."

"We're also facilitating for Ra'id and Amineh," he said.

"In what way?" She looked up from setting rocks on the children's sketches so they wouldn't blow away if the wind came up.

Zafir's dry lift of his brows made the wheels roll and click in her head. But he couldn't really be saying what she thought he was saying. They were having sex?

"You're like one of those chameleons that switches color between one breath and the next." His husky tone laughed at her flush.

"Well, I can't believe what you just implied! It's rather personal, isn't it? And she's your sister. Did they actually *ask* you…?"

"*No*. And I'm not going to dwell on whether that's what they're really doing. But the girls both have birthdays about nine months after past vacations here. Ra'id has had a killer travel schedule the last few years, but he told me last night they're looking forward to a more settled life next year." He shrugged. "And he loves his girls, but his successor is his brother. He'd like a son."

"What about your son?" she asked tartly. "Also an oasis baby?"

He lost all hint of humor as his expression shuttered. "Wedding night."

Conversation closed, she heard loud and clear. It left her feeling as though she'd overstepped, but he started it.

The children returned and they headed out. Twenty minutes later, they had followed a track through tall grass that crackled like green flames around them, then they climbed to a vantage point above the spring. Zafir explained the relay station that kept them in contact with the outside world and the girls waved at the servants in the camp below.

No sign of Ra'id and Amineh. That shouldn't make her feel envious, but Fern was. Greener than the oasis.

We all have different paths, Miss Ivy would say. *Bloom where you're planted*. She was full of those sorts of sayings. Most of the time Fern appreciated that encouraging, make-the-best-of-it quality in her friend. Today she just felt…single.

Disregarded.

Unloved and unlovable.

Zafir showed the children how to use his digital camera then stepped back to watch them stalk geckos in the rocks.

Fern stood a few feet away, looking over the camp below. Her narrow waist was emphasized by the wide band of her beige skirt and her arms were covered by an equally dull-colored shirt, but his mind kept seeing her as she'd looked this morning: a water nymph sent to inflame him. She'd risen from the water, small breasts high and firm and topped by pebbled nipples he'd longed to tongue and suck. Her form was sleek, her femininity understated, but she'd been undeniably all woman when the fabric of her nightgown had painted her stomach and upper thighs, falling away into a frustrating veil that hid her most intimate flesh.

He'd already been primed for her, having spent the night recalling those confusing moments in her tent. She'd been such a curious mixture of invitation and hesitation, baffling him. Experienced women could be notorious teases, but he hadn't caught that vibe from her. More an alarmed hesitation that had stopped him as much as the knowledge that kissing her at all was reckless.

He'd been so sure she was feeling the attraction as strongly as he was, but she'd tripped away like a frightened rabbit. He didn't prey on women so her reaction had made him feel like a cad.

Her faltering made sense now that he understood how inexperienced she was, but through the night he'd pulled his own insecurities into the equation and tortured himself by wondering whether she really wanted him. The idea that she didn't, when he burned for her so strongly, had been painful. Really, truly agonizing.

And then she'd stood before him in the pool and projected all those signals of yearning again, her body on display. He'd had to know.

Her lips had latched to his as she surrendered to passion and that had been it. He couldn't remember a time when a simple kiss had ignited him so thoroughly. They were a perfect match and only the knowledge that his and Ra'id's men were watching over them had kept him from giving in to the barbarian ancestry that had raged to the fore. He'd trembled with the effort to keep from pressing her back onto the dry sand, lifting her night dress and filling her with the flesh that had thickened in powerful response to the sight of her.

Getting her into his tent and under him had been imperative.

And if she had agreed, he would have breached her maidenhead.

That still confounded him. Her reluctant "of course I want to" had been ringing in his head since she'd said it, soothing his ego. It now offered bittersweet consolation as he faced that he really couldn't seduce her. It would be the height of dishonor.

Why couldn't she be the sophisticate that most of her countrywomen were?

"Tell me about yourself, Fern," he commanded, still not fully believing what she'd revealed. "Have you never been curious?"

She flashed him a startled, slightly harassed look, then glanced at the children working out a rotation system for the camera. Tariq's guard had wandered farther up the path and beyond their hearing.

"I'm highly curious," she argued with small flags of pink on her cheekbones. "For instance, I wonder why Tariq's guard came with us but none to watch the girls. What conclusion should I draw from that?"

"My son's guard is our best snake handler," he replied with amusement, more than aware his culture was still quite sexist by Western standards, but in this case his reasons were purely practical. "I thought it wise to have him scout the area before letting the children poke around. Now stop evading my question. You know what I'm really asking. How old are you? If you were from this part of the world I wouldn't be surprised, but how does an English girl remain untouched until she's twenty-two?"

"Three," she countered with a little grimace and a defensive fold of her arms. She pushed her straw hat more firmly onto her head, no doubt trying to hide beneath its wide brim. "I had other priorities," she said. "And it's not something I want to throw away out of mere curiosity."

She sounded prudish and uptight, not like a typical product of the Western world. Male or female, most people her age were hooking up out of boredom if nothing else. He'd been a kid in a candy store at that age, having developed some skill by his early twenties and feeling the pressure to marry soon. He'd taken advantage of every opportunity while he'd had his freedom.

Good thing he had, since his married years had been dry.

"That wasn't meant to sound like a challenge," she added, sending him a look he supposed was intended as a rebuff, but as he held her gaze, her expression softened to yesterday's absorption.

She didn't realize it, but that mixed signal of defensiveness and yearning challenged him to show her what she was missing. Just touching her bare arm had filled him with excitement. Something more could be truly volatile and he was darkly tempted to discover the extent of it.

"There are other ways to find pleasure without going all the way," he pointed out, mind already several hundred meters down that road with her. "I'm having trouble believing you're so inexperienced you've never been kissed."

"I didn't say that," she retorted. "Just that I haven't—" Pain flashed across her expression and she fixed her attention on the children. "I'm no supermodel. Men don't find me interesting."

Her bruised confidence got to him. It made him soft and weak when he needed to be strong and resistant, but he understood the feeling of being spurned better than most. Her lack of self-assurance wasn't something he could ignore and allow to grow like a cancer.

"Don't underestimate yourself. Men are lazy and will pick the lowest-hanging fruit. It doesn't mean the apples higher up aren't appealing."

"Says the man who turned up his nose at the only fruit in the bowl this morning," she retorted, then went red. "Ignore that. You're right. Let's forget all of this. It makes me feel ridiculous."

Such a quick, defensive reaction suggested he'd hit a nerve. Her insecurity went deeper than he'd realized. That made him uncomfortable. He ought to let her think he had rejected her and leave it at that, but he couldn't.

"I covered you this morning because I didn't want other men seeing what I want for myself. You *have* my interest, Fern," he admitted.

His words snapped her head around, her shocked face framed in the brim of her silly hat. A vulnerable softness that was appealing and very temptingly receptive edged into her eyes.

He reached for what little control he had, which was surprisingly tenuous.

"But do you know anything about our history?" His low tone came out aggressive and rough, colored by lifelong bitterness at the hurdles put in front of him by the accident of his birth and now the addition of this…denial of something he wanted quite badly.

"My father's affair with my mother caused a huge rift in our country. He called off his arranged marriage, flaunted his half-breed son as his heir. Any hint of my Western upbringing is seen as a flaw by my detractors. If we were in London, I would seduce you into my bed right this second, but we're not. So even though one of my favorite things in the world is finding wild strawberries in a field, for the sake of my country and quite possibly my life, you and I can't happen."

His words poured lava through her arteries. Not the part where he made it clear the consequences of sleeping with her really might be dire, but the part where he acted like he truly wanted to. That made sensuous feelings pool into her loins as a hot, heavy ache turned her into the ripe fruit he was talking about. *Reach for me. Consume me.*

She couldn't look away from him and didn't know how to hide the effect he had on her. With a kind of desperation, she searched to be sure there was no laughter or subterfuge in his expression and only saw his pupils flare.

Her heart skipped.

"What kills me is knowing *you* have options," he said in a begrudging growl, flicking a glance toward Tariq's guard. "Several."

"What?" She glanced at the man who was nudging beneath a stunted bush with a long stick. "I'm not attracted to him! Not to any of the men."

"Only me?" he challenged, but even though there was a hint of belligerence in his tone, it was a statement, one that made him nod once in satisfaction. "Good."

"No, it's not!" she said loudly enough to make the children stop and look toward them.

Fern crossed her arms, annoyed with herself, but Zafir easily excused her outburst.

"Miss Davenport is taking issue with my calling England soggy. She doesn't realize I'm speaking with the affection of a countryman." Turning back to her, he contradicted quietly, "If you began visiting other men's tents, I don't think I would react very well."

"I don't… What does that mean? You'd be…" She couldn't make herself say it. It would be reaching way beyond her grasp and she'd fall on her face.

"Jealous?" Zafir suggested through teeth set in a dangerous smile. "It's worse than that. My ego likes knowing you react only to me. It's not civilized, but only half of me is English. The other half is centuries-old barbarian. I want you, but if I can't have you, no one else can."

Her brain was doing three-sixties, stunned by his arrogance, cursing her inability to disguise her attraction, and some wicked part of her was deeply thrilled by his seeming possessiveness. It made her realize exactly how seductive it was to feel wanted by the person who intrigued you.

On the other hand… "This is ludicrous," she muttered. "No one has ever… I *am* completely English. Is this how you talk to every woman you meet?" She was blushing—of course she was—but she was indignant enough to feel her spine lock into place. "Because I can't believe you're acting as if this is…something that could really happen. *I barely know you.*"

"But the way you look at me says I can have

you. I *want* to have you," he warned, looking every inch the desert warrior who stole women for his harem and kept every single one of them pleasured.

A swirl of excitement spiraled downward from her throat to sting her breasts, coil in her abdomen and end as a spark between her thighs. It was a promise of something that had eluded her all her life and she wanted to hang on to it, kindle it and watch it glow hotter.

"You could help me out," he said with a feral growl, nostrils flaring. "Tell me I'm wrong. Refuse me."

She opened her mouth, knowing she should, but he stood there so commandingly. This wasn't about her being too shy or intimidated to assert herself. It was about her being an honest person who was overwhelmed with attraction for the first time in her life. She wasn't a victim of her own urges or his aggression. She finally felt alive and wanted to embrace everything about this glorious awareness.

So not a good idea.

She lifted a hopeless hand. "I told you men don't come on to me. How much experience do you think I have with refusing one?"

He bit out an old-fashioned English curse, one she supposed was apropos, and turned away, too athletic to lurch, but his movements were jerky as he joined the children and admired the shots they'd taken so far.

Fern forced her gaze to the footprints he'd left behind, fearful that she was more like her mother than she'd ever be able to bear.

CHAPTER THREE

"THANKS FOR STAYING behind with me, Fern. This has been a nice day."

Fern couldn't help a small snort as she lifted her eyes off the book she was reading on her tablet. "We've barely done anything. I feel like I'm taking advantage, having such a lazy day."

"Oh, don't be silly. This trip isn't just about Zafir wanting to ensure he has the backing of the nomads. It's a holiday." Amineh came up on her elbow on the mat next to Fern's. "Speaking of the men, I could tell you were curious. Do you wish you'd gone with them?"

"I've never seen anyone hunt with falcons," Fern lied, hoping it was a sufficient excuse for the temptation she'd revealed when Tariq had invited her to join him, his father and Ra'id. Every cell in her body was begging to be near Zafir, but after a glance into his inscrutable expression, she'd declined and had spent the day feeling his absence. "It seemed like male-bonding time, though. And I'd probably cry if they caught something."

That made Bashira look up with a giggle from where she was building a sand castle with her sister. They all looked exactly as they did when they spent occasional afternoons beside the shaded pool at the palace. Amineh wore her bikini and Fern her one-piece. They'd waited until the sun had lowered enough to create a strip of shade for them to lie upon without needing sunscreen.

"The question is, do *you* wish you were with the men," Fern teased. "You've been glued to your husband since we arrived." It had been four days and while Fern had had the children for a few hours every morning and afternoon, the adults tended to keep their distance, as did Fern. It was the only way she could disguise her fascination with Zafir, but her attraction toward him had only increased rather than abated.

"I'm sorry, Fern—" Amineh began.

"Oh, please don't apologize. You've said before how much you miss your husband when he's traveling or tied up with other things. I'm glad you finally have time together. It's nice."

"It is nice," Amineh agreed. "Glorious," she added on a luxuriant sigh as she settled onto her back, mouth curved into a smugly reminiscent smile.

Her contentment made Fern think that Zafir was probably right about what the couple was doing in their own time. It made Fern long to ask what it was like.

She was sinfully curious to know what it would be like with Zafir. At night she practically called to him with her body, aching for him to come to her and show her everything he'd hinted at. By day she was tortured with angst, trying to fight her obsession while hoarding the little details the children inadvertently dropped about him, wishing she could find something wrong with him that would turn her off, but he seemed to be everything she admired in a person: honest and fair and smart.

The worst part was, he'd said the consequences wouldn't be worth an affair, but all she could think was that she didn't care. She would never meet another man like him. Making love with him would probably push a self-destruct button on her future, making it impossible for any other man to ever live up to the bar Zafir set, but part of her was willing to take that risk. She knew she would always regret it if she didn't.

So irresponsible.

"I should still be a better friend," Amineh said. "Especially since you haven't abandoned me for my brother, which every other female acquaintance has done at one time or another."

"I can barely hold my own with Tariq," Fern muttered, ducking her eyes to her tablet to keep from revealing how quickly she would turn her back on Amineh if Zafir crooked his finger.

"Ra'id likes that you're reserved. He had misgivings about bringing a Western woman into our household. He was afraid there'd be..." She lifted her head to glance at the children, checking to see how closely they were listening, but they were debating the position of a flag. "Politics," she announced with a significant quirk of her mouth. "So don't wish yourself to be different. We like you exactly as you are."

Fern smiled at Amineh, touched. "And that is why you are already a wonderful friend. You make me feel comfortable being who I am. Thank you."

Amineh's compliment was the counterbalance Fern needed to her silly illusions about Zafir. It reinforced that she was better off keeping a low profile and continuing to resist his pull. Her employment and her friend's respect mattered far more than scratching an itch with a man who couldn't offer her a future, she reminded herself.

Mother would be so proud, Fern mentally chided herself sourly.

An hour later, a male voice said something in Arabic that made Amineh gasp and the girls cry, "Baba! You're back! Where is Tariq?"

Fern's heart took flight as she looked for Zafir, but it was only Ra'id. She missed his response as he answered the girls while kissing their heads. The girls looked toward the trail to where the camels were kept and Ra'id added something about "Uncle" so Fern concluded Zafir and Tariq had hung back.

"Miss Davenport," Ra'id greeted with the sparest of acknowledgments before he dropped to sit next to his wife. He set one proprietary hand on Amineh's hip as he leaned in to kiss her with unapologetic thoroughness.

Fern rose to fling her sarong around her waist and begin gathering her things.

"Oh, Fern, you don't have to rush away," Amineh protested breathlessly.

"It's your family time," Fern said, trying not to look too flustered even though she was fighting a stab of envy so deep she could barely speak. "And I should prep for tomorrow's lesson." *Because I'm a spinster schoolmarm who will never have what you have.* Her heart wrenched in her chest as she acknowledged that she did want what Amineh had. Badly. So badly.

"You've embarrassed her, being all sexy like that," Amineh chided, nose-to-nose with her husband.

"Can't be helped. All I've been thinking about since we saw you from the plateau is getting down here to kiss you." He kissed her again, making Amineh release a stifled moan.

Fern walked away, deeply self-conscious, trying not to be obvious as her gaze traveled to the top of the canyon wall. What had Zafir thought when he had looked down on her? she wondered. He hadn't rushed to see her, so apparently she didn't hold the same allure.

Oh, stop it. Of course she didn't. She *had* to shake this preoccupation with him. It wasn't healthy.

She reached her tent and dropped her bag in front of it, then went to the side where she was using the wires as a clothesline. She hung her damp towel then swept her sarong from her waist and shook out the sand.

"Fern." *Zafir.*

Snapping her head up, she pressed a hand to where her heart nearly left her chest.

His shadow came around the side of the tent and his expression tightened when he saw her. He took in her swimsuit and the colorful sarong dangling from her loosened fingers.

Contradictory messages went through her. Habits of a lifetime urged her to cover herself, but a more overpowering weakness held her still for his inspection. Her body tingled under his gaze. Yearning to please stripped her naked to her soul. She was behaving shamelessly, standing here like this without making any attempt at modesty, thinking of all the ways he'd ravished her in her mind, but she did it anyway.

Did he know what she dreamed about?

She looked into his eyes and felt a delicious kick of desire right into her belly. He did. The magnetic pull she felt toward him was visceral. He grew bigger before her eyes as he drew in a hissing breath, chest expanding—

He grasped her arms, overwhelming her as he walked her backward to the tiny strip of sand behind her tent.

She pressed her hands into his chest, more for balance, alarmed by how quickly and easily he'd taken control of her, yet incredibly weak. He wasn't being rough. There was nothing forceful in his handling of her. She capitulated like her bones were sand and her muscles melted wax.

When she felt the powdery give of sand beneath her back, she had another moment of thinking *do something*, but Zafir was looking at her mouth and her lips were searing with need. She licked them and he swooped to kiss her. She responded by parting her lips and moving them against his.

A punch of pure desire went into her middle as the kiss deepened like a fall into an abyss. Her buckling arms fell away from between them. She splayed her hands on his rib cage and began lightly kneading to learn his form through the folds of his *thobe*. When his tongue flicked into her mouth, she dashed her own against his and white light flashed through her. The pressure of his mouth increased and she welcomed it, opening more for him, not able to breathe but not caring.

His hand slid up her arm to her shoulder and cupped her neck, and the weight of his thumb almost seemed to urge her to calm. Like he was reassuring her they had time. He would be here a while. They didn't have to kiss each other to death this second.

She relaxed and his mouth played with hers, nipping, sucking at her lips, feasting on her, filling her with liquid pleasure, making her arch up to his big body, seeking more contact.

He made a growling noise and his knee came between hers and parted her legs in a way that was so shockingly proprietary she opened her eyes. He lifted his head and watched as he peeled the strap of her suit off her shoulder until her small, pale breast was revealed.

Oh, please, she thought, when she really should have been thinking and acting far more sensibly, but the avid light in his gaze made her feel pretty and wanted. Her nipple prickled, anticipating his touch. Aching for it. This was everything she'd been fantasizing about. More.

He traced light fingers over her skin, watching as he tickled the swell, grazed the underside then settled his hand in a light cup. Hot. His hand was so hot on her cool, damp skin. When he drew his finger and thumb together in a delicate pinch of her nipple, the sensation was so sharp and exquisite, she could only open her mouth in a silent scream.

He bent again, this time capturing her nipple with his masterful lips, burning her like a brand and making her twist in confusion at how flagrant this was. Daylight. Barely hidden from view. It was a familiarity she'd dreamed of, but hadn't realized that it would make her belly knot with pulses of pleasure. Heat flooded into her loins, creating an ache that made her want to beg. Her fingers went into his hair under his *gutra*, but the feel of it was so sensual and spiky and masculine, she could only massage his scalp in encouragement, pushing the headdress off, wanting this to last forever.

His hand scalded the top of her thigh, slid low and pressed to open her legs wider so he could cover her mound with his burning hand.

"Zafir," she moaned, dying at how bold he was being, yet it felt incredible. Hot and *oh*… Streaks of pleasure rocketed into her thighs.

His mouth came back to hers, kissing her deeply, capturing her shaken breaths. "Shh," he breathed and licked her neck under her ear. "Lift into my hand. Show me what you like."

She couldn't. Didn't even know how. But somehow her hand went over his and she pressed and arched and dug the back of her head into the sand as sensations glittered through her. She writhed with abandon under his provocative touch, dying at how flagrantly she was behaving, but she'd been thinking about this and wanting it and it was so much better in real life.

They kissed again and again. She could feel his erection against her hip and rubbed, finding a rhythm with him that built the sensations. This was what lovemaking felt like, she distantly thought. Like heaven. Like nothing else in the world mattered except continuing to do this until they reached their nameless destination.

He shifted his hand, fingertips sliding along the edge of her bathing suit and pushing it aside so she was naked to his touch.

She gasped and turned her head into his shoulder, breaking their kiss as she dealt with the reality of knowing she was as naked and brazen as a woman could be. She looked up at him with alarm, certain she'd find judgment there.

"You're so close. Let me." His hot breath caressed her lips and his fingertip eased along her center and parted her flesh with a stunning sensation that stole any willpower she had. She let him trace back and forth and explore her in a way that was so mesmerizing she had to close her eyes, but that made the feelings all the more acute.

"Oh," she gasped softly as a particularly sharp sensation pierced her.

She felt him smile against her mouth, but her focus narrowed to only his touch, delicate and certain, pressing, circling, rubbing and rubbing, drawing her closer and tighter to the edge of reason, making her scalp tighten—

"Oh, Zafir—" He covered her mouth as the sob built in her throat, reminding her to hold it back as he slid his finger into her and made her world shatter.

She clung to him, overwhelmed by the cataclysm. Nothing in her sheltered little world had prepared her for how amazing he made her feel. Delicious convulsions of joy rocked through her, settling her in a place where nothing existed but him, his touch, his kiss.

The sensations went on and on, slowly fading and leaving her in a floaty place where she felt closer to him than she'd ever felt to another human being. A distant part of her was aware that he was still fondling her, soothing her down from the clouds in the most intimate way, but it felt natural and delicious and she wanted to stay right here luxuriating in—

"Miss Davenport? Are you in there?"

Tariq.

They jerked apart and her hands automatically scrambled her swimsuit back into place. *What had she just done?*

Zafir nudged her to rise and she flashed him a look, cut by the grim scowl he wore. He mouthed *Answer*.

"I'm, um, yes, I'm here, Tariq." She grabbed her sarong off the ground and wrapped it around herself, trying not to hang herself on the wires as she glanced back to ensure Zafir wasn't visible. "What did you need?"

"Did my father come see you?"

"Um…" Her brain blanked, unable to conjure a lie even to a child when it was critically necessary.

"To invite you to eat with us tonight?" Tariq prompted.

"Oh! Was your, um, hunt successful?"

"Just three birds, but it's enough. Are you coming swimming? Walk with me. I'll tell you about it."

"I've been swimming already. I need to rest now." Take cover. Regroup. She couldn't believe what she had just let happen.

"You should cool off in the water," he suggested. "You look hot."

She blushed harder as she thought of the reason she looked overheated.

"Good advice," she choked. "I'll think about it

and join you in a minute." There. Finally a credible lie.

As Tariq ran off, Fern stood there in bewilderment. Her blood still sang and her skin felt like it was made of velvet. Forget swimming. She was so lethargic, she could barely stay on her feet, but she was gripped by mortification so intense she was terrified to move.

Glancing around the camp, she saw no one who might have seen what she'd been doing, where she'd been, or with whom. Was he still there?

Ducking into her tent, she went to the back wall and whispered, "Are you still there?"

Nothing. When she looked out the screen that formed a small window in the back wall, she saw no one. It was both a relief and a disappointment. Going back outside, she went behind the tent and kicked sand across the impression they'd left with their rolling, then scrubbed her bare foot over the man-sized sandal prints that disappeared into the forest of grass and palm trees behind her tent.

Two days ago, she'd snuck his towel into the latrine and left it on a hook. For someone who didn't know how to be deceptive, she was becoming very duplicitous.

The full impact of what she'd just done with Zafir began to hit her. Before this it had been a kiss and a conversation. Now...

She wouldn't let herself savor how it had felt.

He'd had his hands on her in places she felt guilty touching herself!

She was entering the territory her mother had always warned her about. Behavior that was dangerous and had no future. She could hide the evidence, but she couldn't deny that clothing had been moot and inhibition nonexistent. He'd held her in the palm of his hand, literally. He'd driven her to a point of supreme vulnerability and helplessness and she hadn't fought him because nothing in her had wanted to.

Her mother had names for women who acted this way. Fern burned with humiliation at the thought of Zafir labeling her the same way. Where was her self-respect?

How would she ever face him again?

Zafir was suffering like a man staked on an anthill in the desert. His skin prickled, his core was on fire, he couldn't fight his way free of the situation he was in and regret sat like dust in the back of his throat because all of this was his own fault. He should have left Fern alone.

His control had been holding up well, even though he was aware of her every move in the camp. Even though her voice sometimes carried to him and he felt so drawn he shook with the effort to ignore her. When she'd looked to him as his son had invited her to spend the day in the desert with them, hunting the falcons, he had willed her to refuse.

She had, and his inner being had screamed like a hawk, angry that she had denied herself to him.

It made no sense. He barely knew her and was making every effort to remain estranged, but he'd thought of her the entire time they were hunting. He had easily imagined her inquisitive, engaging manner and pictured her freckled face turned to the sky in anticipation. He'd wanted her to see his desert and this ancient practice and be a part of his world in this elemental way.

Why?

Aside from his wife, he'd never attached himself to any woman and even that had been...

He ducked thoughts of his marriage as he always did, instead comparing Fern to some of his much more pleasant, lengthier affairs. Pretty, sensuous women who purred under his touch. But he'd never felt more than mild inconvenience when those relationships ended. If a new female in his sphere caught his eye, but turned out to be married or otherwise unavailable, he easily transferred his interest elsewhere.

So why couldn't he dismiss Fern? Was it because no other choices were open to him, as she'd accused him?

His marriage had lasted nearly five years and he'd gone without sex *that* long. A fortnight without a woman ought to be well within his endurance level.

But Fern's hold on him was unprecedented. When they'd returned to the oasis and looked down on the camp, Tariq had said Miss Davenport looked a skeleton on the sand. Ra'id had chuckled and Zafir had had to bite back a sharp remark, managing to remind his son in a measured tone that he should be more respectful.

Yes, she had been pale and leggy, but like a piece of carved ivory. Her hair had been a rope of red-gold, hanging in a plait against her back. All he'd thought about the rest of the descent was wrapping it around his fist and holding her for his kiss.

Trying to get a grip on his libido before he saw her, he'd hung back with Tariq to watch him dress the birds they'd caught. After a few moments, his son had said, "I can do it" with that hint of exasperated annoyance children had when a parent hovered. Rather than take offense, Zafir had accepted that he was being a coward. He had gone to relay Tariq's invitation to dinner, then found himself following Fern across the camp.

He should have called out sooner and spoken to her in the open, but the male animal in him had fixated on the twin cheeks that were not voluptuous, but were lovely, firm lobes that moved under the tissue-thin veil of her sarong. Her ambling walk had been lazy. The way she had craned her neck had spoken of her enjoyment in her surroundings.

That sensuous streak was his undoing. His thoughts had turned to how she would react to other physical pleasures. When he'd finally caught up to her in the relative privacy at the side of her tent, he'd already been so primed that her near nudity had devastated what little self-discipline he'd had left. He hadn't even spoken to her. It was a wonder he'd taken the time to press her out of sight before he'd fallen on her.

If only she had recoiled from his touch, but the responsiveness in her was not only a frustrating thrust of responsibility totally onto him, but also pure seduction. When she'd opened her mouth and kissed him back, he'd lost it. His one and only glimmer of sanity had been a recollection that they could be discovered at any second.

And now that he knew how reactive she was, how she melted under his touch and abandoned herself to his lovemaking, he could think of nothing but touching her again. Arousing her to that same level of wildness and thrusting into her. Making her cry her elation into his ear.

So impossible.

Especially as she sat across from him, her lashes lowered, her tongue sweeping her lips between bites of stew. The children bandied for her attention. Even Amineh was determined to engage her.

He did everything he could to avoid even looking at her.

But he noticed Fern had buttoned herself into cotton armor and was acting like she was sitting on a pin. Her hair was hidden under a scarf. Its edges fluttered around her face and she kept touching her collar and tugging her skirt to cover her shin, trying to hold her own against the breeze that had come up as the sun had gone down.

His friend Ra'id could caress his wife's cheek, but he, Zafir, could not reach across and tuck an errant strand of hair under his lover's scarf. The injustice—and the intensity of oppression he felt at being denied—confounded him.

"You've been in such owly moods this trip," his sister said with a nudge of her elbow into his side. "What's bothering you?"

Ra'id covered Amineh's hand and murmured, "Men in our position can't always talk about the concerns we shoulder."

Amineh's gaze flicked to Fern, and Fern was sharp enough to get the message that she had just been labeled an outsider. Her mouth tightened in a tiny flinch, but she quickly hid it behind a smile for Tariq.

"I must thank you again, young man. This has been such a treat. Both the delicious meal and dining with your family. I find such a lively table a bit overwhelming to be honest. It was always just my mother and I growing up. She often worked late so eating alone feels very normal to me."

I won't be insulted if you don't invite me again, her chipper remark seemed to say. *In fact, I'd prefer it.*

It tugged an unexpected pang from Zafir's heart. Ra'id wasn't a snob, but he was a realist. Fern's position in his household was well defined and it behooved all of them to remember it.

Fern started to draw back and excuse herself, but Tariq asked in his direct way, "Where was your father? Did he die?"

"No, um…" Fern widened her eyes like she'd stepped into unexpected traffic. "I mean…" She swallowed.

"Parents don't always live together," Amineh ventured, sending an empathetic look to Fern who was looking at Ra'id with deep shame, like she expected him to banish her to the edges of the earth for daring to be illegitimate in front of his daughters. Obviously she was forgetting that the girls' mother and uncle were bastards.

"Like grandmother stayed in England, rather than live here?" Bashira asked.

"Exactly," Amineh said, setting a hand on her daughter's head while she flashed a long-suffering look toward Zafir.

Being the product of an unwed union wasn't something they talked about often, and neither of them had found the best way to dig deep into the topic with their children, but it was a scar they both carried. It shouldn't matter in this day and age, but he still faced bigotry every day from certain factions in his country, for being illegitimate and half blood, making it impossible for him to forget he was not wholly a product of his own country.

And there was Fern looking like she shared the same agony at being born on the wrong side of the blanket.

You're in good company, he wanted to blurt, but she was rallying, mustering a smile. "Thank you again. I wish I could offer to make you some traditional English food, Tariq, but I think you've probably tried all of it with your grandmother."

"She won't let the chef make fish and chips. That's my favorite. Sometimes Baba and I sneak out for it."

"State secrets revealed after all," Fern murmured, then bit her lips together. Her face darkened in the glow of the candles as she rose jerkily from her cushion and bowed to take her leave.

"No, don't go," Jumanah urged.

"Listen, I hear the music starting." Fern touched her ear and pointed in the direction of the cooking area. "That means it will be your bedtime soon.

But if your parents allow it, you may come to my tent and we'll see if we can identify some of the constellations from the guide on my tablet before it loses the last of its charge."

"Please, Baba?" the girls begged.

Tariq gave Zafir an excited, expectant look. For a boy who thought she looked like a skeleton and who was on vacation from school, he seemed quite taken with Miss Davenport. Genetics again, Zafir thought, wanting to shake his head at the irony.

"Of course," he said with a nod. "I have a travel unit with several charges left. You can use it to keep your tablet going through the rest of our stay."

"If it's not an imposition," Fern said, flashing him a slightly fraught glance. It was the first and only direct eye contact of the night and burned a trail through him like a comet.

"I'll get it," Tariq said, leaping to his feet.

Fern's shoulders softened with relief and she herded the children into the shadows toward her tent.

"Well, that was the height of awkward," Ra'id said in Arabic.

"Oh, don't start!" Amineh protested, throwing her weight into her husband.

He caught her close as he chided, "Be honest. Have you ever seen anyone that uncomfortable for two solid hours? It was painful. Wasn't it, Zafir?"

"You don't realize how intimidating you are! Zafir, too. And she's not a talkative person. That's why I like her. There's no gossipy 'Did you hear this or that?' She talks about real things."

"Such as?" Zafir asked, trying to keep his tone idle as he mentally castigated his son for stealing his one valid excuse to seek her out.

"The girls and their progress, mostly. But she wants to learn about our culture. We both agree the world would be a better place if women ran it," she taunted with a grin up at her husband.

"Goes without saying," Ra'id agreed, kissing her nose.

"You're not bonding over unwed parents, then," Zafir said, recognizing the nuzzling as his cue to make himself scarce.

"Okay, that *was* awkward," Amineh agreed, sitting up a little. "And no, we don't. I gather her mother was a bit of a hard case, but she doesn't go on about it or pry. She's very earnest."

"I'll give you that," Ra'id said, reaching to drain his cup of tea. "I have stacks of picture books awaiting my approval before she reads them to our children. How dangerous a political message could be hidden in a story that wishes the moon a good-night? When she started, she asked me how much of her curriculum she should devote to British history and suggested twenty-five per-cent because the girls are one quarter English."

Zafir didn't want to laugh at her, but he couldn't help the twitch of his lips as he considered the contradiction of the laced-up schoolmistress and the woman who had broken all the rules with him this afternoon. His ego soared with triumph at how much she had let go with him.

"Stop," Amineh insisted to Ra'id. "Or I'll tell her you want to mark all their written work your-self."

They started to snog openly so Zafir pushed to his feet and went to his tent. There he discovered that Tariq had taken his charging unit, but left all the attachments.

His mind said *don't*. His fingers gathered up the velvet bag of adaptors and weighed the pack-age in his palm.

He managed to resist going to her until Tariq came to say good-night. The boy was riding a streak of independence these days, insisting he could scrub his own teeth and put himself to bed. As he rushed off to do so, Zafir stepped outside.

Ra'id was carrying his daughters like rolled car-pets, one giggling girl under each of his arms, to where their mother waited near the children's tent.

Fern stood alone near her own, tablet in hand, face turned to the sky as she moved from beneath the canopy of palms.

As Zafir debated lame excuses to go to her, like asking if he could help her find a particular constellation, without any word to anyone, Fern made a decisive turn and headed up the path he'd taken her and the children a few days ago.

CHAPTER FOUR

FERN'S ANTENNAE PICKED up his presence before she heard or saw him. All the hairs on her body lifted and a jolt of such electric awareness shot through her, she expected her tablet to short out.

She kept walking, heartbeat picking up speed under the sense of being pursued, but she wasn't frightened. Not exactly. He wouldn't hurt her.

But when she finally heard his voice asking, "Where the hell are you going?" his stern undertone was daunting enough to make her halt with apprehension.

She hugged the tablet to her chest like a shield and turned to face him. They were still under the palms at the top of the spring so the filtered light left only a few glinting strips on his face, not enough to read his expression, but she received his message of disapproval loud and clear.

He didn't think she was looking for one of the guards, did he? They were so elusive, she wouldn't know where to find one if she needed one.

"The plateau," she replied, managing a conversational tone. "We couldn't see much of the sky from the camp. I wanted to see if it's worth asking to bring the children up tomorrow night for a proper stargaze."

"You're not allowed to leave the camp without an escort."

That took her aback. "I'm not supposed to take the children out of the camp. No one said I can't go for a walk by myself."

"I'm telling you that you can't. You could fall or get a bite, especially in the dark."

"Are you serious?"

"Completely."

She had read all the stories about stupid tourists getting themselves into sticky situations and didn't fancy becoming one, but his order seemed silly. She huffed, feeling like she was being treated like a child. "Fine. Will you take me?"

A loaded silence was his response.

"I meant—"

"I know what you meant," he growled impatiently.

What did one say to that? She hugged the tablet so tightly her fingers hurt where the edges dug in.

When he moved toward her, she pivoted to the side of the trail, making room for him to take the lead.

He stopped in front of her, hands coming to her

upper arms the way they had this afternoon. His touch was light, but his voice heavy. "Come off the path with me."

"Zafir," she whispered hoarsely, but a pulse of desire expanded in her so hard her entire body hurt. She reminded herself there was no future with him, but the warning carried zero weight against her inner yearning. Even if all she had was his kisses and caresses, it was more than she'd ever imagined for herself.

She wasn't completely senseless, though. She understood one dire consequence she'd be courting if she went with him.

"I don't have anything. I'm not on the pill." The white of his *thobe* filled her blurred vision and the scent of him, dusty and spicy and heady, fogged her senses into a state of capitulation. Was she making assumptions saying that? Looking like a fool? At this point it didn't matter. She'd already bared herself about as much as anyone could, but he needed to know how completely unprepared she was for anything like this.

"I won't make love to you like that," he assured in a voice that gently stripped her of her flimsy defenses, like sensually pulling away silky veils. "Your virginity is for the man you marry. I just want to hold you. Kiss you and touch you like I did this afternoon. You liked it, yes? It was good?"

He sounded like he really wanted to know. Like he couldn't tell? She'd shattered under his touch!

His husky whisper, the feel of his breath stirring her hair, brought it all back so she was exactly as she'd been a few hours ago: completely enthralled by him. She bit back a moan and her head felt too heavy for her neck. Her forehead fell against the hard wall of his muscled chest.

"You're so sweet, Fern. Like honey." He drew her to align with his body so she could feel his arousal through their clothes. She pushed the tablet away from between them and let it fall to the sand. His hands molded her with familiarity even as he shuffled her off the path to a place where they had a measure of privacy.

"This is bad, Zafir. You said so," she reminded.

He only braced his back on a palm trunk and opened his legs to make a space for her. She was burning alive, but she snuggled into his heat, arms encircling his neck like her body knew what it was doing even if she didn't. She angled her head and followed the pressure of his hand in her hair to mate her mouth to his.

So bad and so good. They kissed like long-lost lovers. Maybe he was using her. Maybe she was being fanciful, but this felt like reunion. His hands on her were magic, his mouth divine. The evidence of his desire for her was so mysterious and heartening, she couldn't help pressing into him with gratified joy.

When he pulled her shirt free and stroked her back, she caught back a moan and searched for his skin, but it was impossible to find. The shape of his chest and ribs were hard and wide, enthralling to her splayed fingers, but the cloth of his *thobe* was trapped by the press of their bodies.

He loosened her bra and found her breasts. His knowing hand tenderly caressed her and circled her nipple, making it feel taut and achy. She wriggled her hips into him even more. Oh, she wanted him to suckle at her again.

"Zafir," she said, breaking their kiss to gasp. "I want to feel your skin, too."

He breathed a ragged curse against her lips and set her back a step, pulling up his *thobe* from between them. When she burrowed beneath it and discovered the hot skin of his waist, her hands couldn't get enough. His chest expanded, his abdomen contracted, his chest hair was a fine, intriguing texture traveling in a line downward—

She gasped as she was realized what grazed her wrist. "You're naked under here."

"I am." He opened the button at her throat and moved to the next.

"Can I—"

"Yes."

Looking down but seeing only his sleeve as he

continued opening her buttons and the bunched white cotton draping her own arms, she let her fingers hesitantly explore, blind but curious.

So amazing. His shape was steely under a layer of smooth velvet, and he quivered at her light touch. Taut and aggressive and so thick. She couldn't imagine how men and women fit together when she held the girth and weight of him in her fist.

"Am I doing it right?" she asked in an anxious whisper.

"Harder," he murmured against her lips, cupping both her breasts beneath her loosened bra and then teasing her nipples so she pinched her legs tight against a pulse of heat.

She loved this. Loved feeling him tighten in her hand, loved hearing his breath catch and feeling his tongue delve into her mouth as he kissed her and seemed excited by her touch. If she could give him what he'd given her this afternoon, she'd be overjoyed.

He drew back unexpectedly and she looked into his shadowed face, wondering if it was a trick of the light that his eyelids were so low, his mouth slack with passion.

"What's wrong?" she whispered, loosening her touch on him.

"Nothing." He sounded drugged. "Keep going. It feels good."

He gathered her skirt as he talked. The hem tickled her bare legs, sensitizing her, building anticipation so she throbbed between her thighs. He slouched lower and caught her leg to guide her knee over his muscled thigh, opening her to his touch. Her thigh was scraped by the abrasion of his and she flinched.

"What—?" Off balance, she fell into him, hand squeezing and making him grunt. "I'm sorry! I'm bad at this."

"No, Fern, you're not." He laughed softly against her mouth as he caressed her through her knickers.

Her turned to gasp and pull away a fraction before he could kiss her. "What are you doing?"

"We'll do this together." He tucked his fingers into her underpants and let the cotton trap his hand against her needy flesh.

Her body responded with a rush of liquid heat, clasping with hollow need.

"This is really bad. It has to be," she murmured, thinking, *under the shirt, down the pants*. Nothing good came of this, but it felt incredible.

"Do you want to stop?" His lips played along her jaw, enticing her mouth to catch up to his while her mind was filled with nothing but the delicate stroke of his fingers where she ached and throbbed.

"No," she admitted on a sob, pushing into his hand for a firmer touch.

"Neither do I."

Fern woke to a pleasant awareness of the flesh between her legs and a memory of holding the sun as it went supernova in her hands. Afterward, as they'd leaned there, shaking, his arm locking her to his pounding heart, he'd whispered, "It's probably best we don't go all the way, Fern. It might kill us."

She smiled into her pillow as she thought of it again. The way he'd kissed her after they'd put themselves back together had been incredibly encouraging.

"It's not bad, Fern," he'd promised her. "It's not smart," he admitted in a dry whisper, "but what we're doing isn't sinful. I won't let it go too far. You won't lose your job or get pregnant. I'll be discreet."

"You're saying you want to do this again?"

"Don't you?"

"I do," she'd breathed, massaging the muscles of his back, incredulous that she was in his arms, that he held her so close, that this was even happening. She had pushed aside reservations and worries about being the only fruit in the bowl, focusing instead on the way he kneaded her bottom and seemed reluctant to release her so they could find the things they'd dropped on the path and walk back to camp. He had kept her hand in his until the last moment.

Her mother would call this kind of sneaking around cheap, but even if he was taking advantage of her naiveté and inexperience, he was doing it tenderly. This was the kind of affair she'd always secretly dreamed of. She couldn't imagine regretting it, especially if there weren't any long-term consequences.

That word—*long-term*—made her bite her lip and lick at the sting.

Zafir and Amineh were close, but in the way of adult siblings who lived in two separate countries. They stayed in touch, but didn't spend a lot of time together.

This affair, if it qualified to be called such a thing, would be very short-lived. She had absolutely no future with Zafir, she knew that. Still, she couldn't resist stealing this chance to be intimate with him, not because she wanted to learn about sex, although that was definitely part of it. She also liked feeling desirable and prized. But more than all of that, she wanted to learn about him.

So she wouldn't worry about the future. They had today, Fern assured herself as she pushed up from her bed, already wondering how he would find her and when.

Except the din from the camels that she had put down to one of their cranky periods seemed to be growing and the babble of voices speaking Arabic increased in volume.

Peeking out of her tent, she discovered they were being invaded.

Zafir's father had loved all things Western, to the point that he'd pushed his new ideas too hard and fast on a culture still catching up to the twentieth century and far from ready to embrace the twenty-first. Ra'id's father had been more conservative, which had bequeathed a host of different issues on Ra'id as a leader, but one thing they both needed without question was the support of the Bedouin clan that roamed their lands.

He and Ra'id had come to the oasis specifically to meet with the leader of this tribe and reaffirm their alliance with him. The tribe might stay as long as a week, but Zafir found himself wishing they would hurry themselves along.

Fern was waiting for him. Fern, with her shy touch and eagerness to please and her abandonment to passion. They were behaving like teenagers in the back of a car and it was one of the most exhilarating experiences of his life.

Yet he was back to barely acknowledging her when he glimpsed her walk past with his nieces. She wore her abaya and it had smudges of dust at the wrist, but she still managed to look prim and cute at the same time. Her glorious hair was hidden beneath a black scarf, the curled tip of the tail peeking from the hem on her back. She had pinned a veil across her face so only the freckled bridge of her nose was visible, along with her quiet gray eyes.

Her strawberry-blond lashes had dropped demurely when she'd caught his eye. He could only see that narrow band of her face, but he'd been sure she had blushed.

Because she was remembering.

The memories stoked heat through him, too, filling him with need, but there wouldn't be so much as a conversation between them while the nomads filled the oasis. The servants kept to themselves and his guards might turn a blind eye to his stealing off with her, but he couldn't afford to dent his reputation with people who already mistrusted him for his father's bold antics.

So he kept his distance while discussing where decent range land could still be found and stayed up late, nodding his head to the music and admiring the skills of the sword dancers. When asked, he agreed that yes, he was considering remarrying. No, nothing was formalized, but yes, he would search for his match within his own borders.

He kept to himself that the prospect filled him

with dread. He resented his father for seeking his own pleasure at the expense of not just his country, but his immediate family. Even the woman his father claimed to have loved beyond reason, Zafir's mother, had suffered under his father's selfish pursuit of his own happiness. Zafir refused to commit the same crime. His marriage had been difficult, but he had Tariq from the union and more stability in his country as a result. The sacrifice had been worth it. He would do it again.

But not yet. *After* he left the oasis.

Indulging himself with Fern didn't make him like his father, he reasoned, throwing an arm over his eyes as he lay in bed fighting the urge to go to her. One small dalliance with an English woman on holiday was not the same as sentencing two children—*two*—to a lifetime of conflict in their identity.

Not that he allowed that conflict to continue to rage in him anymore. He was wholly a man of the desert and did his best to prove it, hunting with the men the next day and playing a type of polo on camels the following. If he longed for the sweet yet tart taste of strawberry bursting in his mouth, no one, most especially the forbidden fruit in question, knew.

Until the next afternoon when she stunned him by calling, "Zafir!" and came running toward him across the camp.

His companion, the sheikh of this visiting Bedouin tribe, stopped beside him and swung a look of startled denunciation at Zafir. Who was this girl to act so familiar?

Zafir bristled, accosted by a sensation like his innermost desires, the things he kept most private to himself, had been turned out onto the sand. Like she was jerking back a curtain and crying "he's English, he's mine" exactly when he was needing to be seen at his most independent and Arabic.

And because of that instant sense of exposure and shame in his own weakness, he stopped her with a glare.

She halted and a startled, guarded look came into her eyes as she looked uncertainly between them.

"I mean, abu Tariq," she said, using the more formal address as she took a few hurried steps toward him. Amineh had arranged for Fern to spend time with the Bedouin women, to observe their sewing and weaving, but it really was better if Fern was seldom seen and rarely heard while the nomads were here.

"Not now," he stated flatly and started to turn his friend away, asserting that she was nothing to him.

"It can't wait," she insisted, circling into his line of vision.

He let her see his outrage. If she thought their touchy-feely little tryst entitled her to his attention on her whim, she was dead wrong.

Hurt flashed in her eyes, but even though her slim build seemed to pull tight and become even more narrow, and the little he could see of her face was pale enough to make her freckles stand out in dark spots, she kept her gaze locked with his.

"A girl is ill. Her mother isn't taking it seriously and I can't find your sister. I only have Bashira to interpret."

The man beside him demanded to know what she was saying. Zafir translated, aware exactly how much Western interference was welcomed, especially when it involved women making demands. His friend urged him to let the girl's mother be the judge. He dismissed Fern with a step toward her and a flick of his hand to shoo her away.

The action, not meant to actually strike her, still set Zafir's control on edge. Bigotry was his fatal weakness and Fern was being advised firmly of her insignificant status.

She jerked back a step, trepidation fixing her eyes on the man as she excused, "I wouldn't do this if I wasn't worried—"

The wounded throb in her voice told Zafir she realized how completely she was being disregarded. But where he would have called her meek at any other time, she showed inordinate boldness, straightening her spine, growing a fraction taller and speaking with insistence.

"But her mother doesn't want to talk about it because she, well, the girl looks about thirteen. Her mother thinks she's starting her time. I think it's appendicitis."

"Time...?" Comprehension dawned. "She probably is," he averred. What did he know about these things?

"I've had both and you don't get a fever from puberty," she retorted hotly. "You can't ignore this. *I* can't. Come and see for yourself."

That imperative tone of hers made the other sheikh huff out a noise of impatience.

Fern looked braced for a blow, but she stood her ground and stared hard at Zafir, genuine fear in her eyes as she willed him to do as she asked.

If she was wrong, this would turn out badly.

It might anyway. When he assented with a growl and followed her, the girl's mother was appalled that Fern had brought her daughter's condition to the attention of men, most specifically ones in such exalted positions. She tried to wave them away, scolding Fern thoroughly in loud, rapid Arabic. All the women and girls in the communal tent stared, Zafir's nieces included. The girl was so embarrassed, she started to move to the back of the big lean-to.

The Bedouin sheikh pressed Zafir to come away, telling him to let the women handle things. His vile glare at Fern, sharp with censure and mistrust, didn't abate when he looked at Zafir.

Fern caught at Zafir's sleeve and tugged as the girl failed to get her feet under her. "That is not normal," she insisted. "You have to make them realize."

"You've had your appendix out? Tell me the symptoms," he growled. He crouched to talk to the mother and girl and lifted a hand to stay his companion's arguments as he translated Fern's suspicion.

The girl started to cry and her mother wrapped her arms around her, both of them denying it could be that serious. He understood. Who wanted to need surgery when they were two days by camel to the nearest hospital?

Zafir called on one of his guards who was trained as a medic. The guard wasn't allowed to physically examine the girl, of course, but he agreed that the diagnosis could be correct. The father of the girl was found and the entire family sent by helicopter with the girl for treatment.

Fern buttoned herself into her tent—an act that poked at Zafir's conscience—but if he had just had a girl airlifted to a hospital for menstrual cramps, he was going to look worse than his father for listening to her. His attempt to hide that they had a personal relationship would be moot. An affair was already presumed. He'd be labeled as weak, ruled by the same aberrant crush that had undermined his father's ability to govern well.

An air of tension hung over the camp as they waited word via the relay station. Ra'id and Amineh returned from being in the desert with another group, concerned that they'd seen the helicopter come and go. Zafir explained and Ra'id came to Fern's defense, assuring the Bedouins she wasn't the type to stir up false drama.

Zafir couldn't have argued in her favor. It would have looked suspicious and the fact was, he didn't know her well enough to judge her as knowledgeable or trustworthy.

He only knew he never should have touched her.

"Fern." Amineh's voice woke her to the first fingers of daylight. "Are you awake?"

"Yes." She sat up, eyes gritty, and watched the zip climb on the front of her tent.

Amineh poked her head in. "You were right. It was appendicitis. She had the surgery late last night and will be okay. Can you dress and come out? Her uncle wants to thank you."

Relief lifted a huge weight off her chest. Fern took a big breath and let it out. She'd barely slept, she'd been so worried.

And hurt.

Zafir had been so dismissive, like she didn't know her place. He'd certainly made it clear how much value he placed in her opinions. Her mother was right. Men didn't respect women who were easy.

A few minutes later, after ensuring she was covered to the tips of her fingernails, only her eyes showing, she approached the group of men waiting for her near the nomad's cooking fire.

Zafir was in her periphery. She thought she felt his eyes on her, but didn't look to check. It was probably just her constant awareness of him playing up anyway.

The tribal leader, the man who had tried to convince Zafir not to listen to her, set his palm on his chest, closed his eyes and bowed his head. Through Amineh, Fern expressed her relief that the girl would survive. The nomads spent a short hour packing and were gone before anyone was hungry for lunch.

The rest of the day was quiet, even the children not talking much. The men kicked a football with Tariq and Jumanah down the beach while Bashira settled in to show Fern the clothing she'd made for her doll with the help of one of the Bedouin women. Amineh joined them and sat down next to Fern with a huge sigh.

"*Now* we can relax."

"Be honest," Fern said as Bashira ran off in search of a dress she'd forgotten in her tent. "Did I cause a political disaster?"

"It could have gone south if you'd been wrong, but you weren't. Zafir has to be so careful not to be seen as acting like our father and our father was *so* determined to not just modernize, but Westernize. He tried to settle land rights on the tribes and make them farm it. They're already losing clansmen to cities and steady jobs. Their way of life is hard enough without government eroding it. Seeing Zafir with Ra'id, whose family always respected their rights to migrate, goes a long way. That's why we make a point of meeting here like this. The Bedouins travel so much, and talk to so many different people, their opinion can be the difference between large-scale support or opposition for Zafir."

"And I nearly derailed the whole thing."

"You did the right thing. You know that. In fact, Zafir tells me you earned yourself an offer of marriage for it." Amineh nudged her shoulder into Fern's.

"What?" Zafir had told Amineh about them? And he wanted to—

"From the cousin of the girl you saved," Amineh continued, her grin widening. "I guess this young man heard you were learning to weave and that the children liked you. He saw you have red hair, which intrigued him. You've already had your appendix out, so that will never be an issue…" She gurgled the last words with great humor.

That was *not* where she had thought Amineh was going. Mortified by how her hopes had soared under such a wrong assumption, especially when Zafir wasn't even speaking to hcr, Fcrn could only look at the ground as an enormous blush flooded into her cheeks.

Amineh burst out laughing and called down the beach to the men, "I told you she'd turn red as a fire engine!"

Fern tried to act like she saw the humor in it, but she was achingly aware that she was secretly dreaming for more with Zafir when the hard fact was, Amineh had just outlined to her how completely wrong she was for him. Not worth the consequences, he'd said that first morning, and no doubt that had been reinforced for him by yesterday's events.

Assuring herself it was for the best, that furthering their physical intimacy would only set her up for a broken heart, she maintained her distance, ate alone and was in a surprisingly sound sleep when she woke to a hand over her mouth.

CHAPTER FIVE

"It's me. Don't scream."

His whisper, scented faintly of cloves and anise, caressed her cheek.

Belated shock went through her and she jerked her limbs into reacting. Unfortunately he was half on her bedroll, pinning her sheet and keeping her reflexive movements muted. She couldn't even wriggle as he settled his weight half over her.

"Shh. Don't make any noise. I just want to talk."

Forcing herself to stillness, she tried to ignore the way her body blossomed against his, even with his *thobe*, a sheet and her nightgown between. Her breasts tingled, her thighs grew restless. Desire concentrated in her loins, anticipating his touch.

And her helplessness at her own reaction made tears burn her eyes. She turned her head away from him, dislodging his hand from her mouth.

His fingers curled under and he smoothed her

cheek with his knuckle. "I know I was harsh to you," he said tightly. "This thing between us—"

"Is nothing. I know," she asserted, not wanting to hear him say it. "I'm weak, not stupid. I wasn't trying to stake a claim on you. I wasn't assuming we're friends or anything else. We don't even know each other."

His touch stalled, then his breath clouded against her ear in a drained sigh. "I know you're willing to put everything on the line for the life of a girl you barely know." His touch caressed from below her ear, along her jaw and down. He opened his hand on her throat and aligned his thumb along the artery throbbing with needy anticipation. "Thank you for doing that. I couldn't sleep, knowing you thought I was angry with you for it."

She knew she ought to say something. Forgive him. Tell him to go. All she could think about, however, was how it would feel if he slid his hand down to her breast.

"That's all I came for," he said, lifting his hand off her as he started to roll away.

"Is it?" Weak, weak Fern. She closed her eyes against the clamor inside her, the yearning that was so self-destructive as to invite more of his dispassionate lovemaking.

His breath hissed in. He set his hand on her stomach. "You want me to stay?"

She shouldn't. She knew that. But she slid her hand from under the sheet, covered his and lightly drew it up to her breast. "I know it's bad," she whispered achingly.

"I'm the one behaving badly, Fern." He took up her hand and brought her fingers to his lips. "Your first lover should be someone who offers more than a week of stolen rendezvous in the dark. I'm very conscious that I'm taking advantage of you."

She heard the confirmation that this was all they had and it cracked a wide fissure through her. Turning her hand in his, she traced the smooth shape of his lips, aching for better words to come out of them.

"Apparently I have a suitor if I want marriage," she said, smiling sadly and glad he couldn't see it. "At first I thought you were him, here to kidnap me into the desert."

"That's not funny." His grip on her hand tightened and he leaned over her, lips questing for hers. "I wanted to knock his young ass into the dirt when he asked about you. I told you before that if I can't have you, no one can."

"But you can," she told him, smoothing her fingers over the scuff of his growing beard and into his hair to explore the shape of his skull. A distant part of her already wept at the idea of losing him in a few short days, but his possessiveness healed the fracture in her chest with crooked, stinging stitches. Oh, how she wanted this. Him.

His hot mouth caressed the side of her face and she turned her mouth into his, unable to resist.

He muffled a groan and she felt his chest swell. She wondered if it meant he was feeling what she was: heart exploding into faster pounds, nerve endings snapping to life with a pulse of acute need.

She closed her fist to begin bunching his *thobe* behind his shoulders and he lifted to peel her sheet down. Then he reared back on his knees to shed his tunic. His sculpted form was barely visible in the dull purple light inside the tent, a vague silhouette that was undeniably masculine in its size. Powerful. Weakeningly beautiful.

Fern did something she never imagined herself able to do. She shimmied her nightgown up and over her head, tossing it away, then slid her own knickers off and kicked them to the floor as she opened her arms to him.

He fell on her and they kissed and clung like drowning victims. She knew it was bad to wrap her legs around him, but oh, it felt good to feel his aggressive sex rubbing against hers. He thrust his tongue into her mouth, telling her what he wanted to do to her, and she couldn't help releasing a moan of encouragement.

"Shh, *albi*. We have to be quiet." He nibbled

down her neck, sending prickles of excitement through her chest, making her nipples stand taut and sensitive to the friction of his chest hair.

"I know, but it's so hard," she gasped, seeking with her hands for the shape of him. *So* hard.

He muffled a curse against her skin and slid lower, away from her reach as he captured her nipple in his mouth and teased her mercilessly.

"Zafir," she protested, knee coming up in reaction to the jab of sensation his erotic suckling drove into her center.

He only skimmed his hand along her inner thigh, his teeth sinking in lightly around her nipple as his touch slid easily against her ready flesh. She arched in blinded reaction to his caress and he deepened his exploration, pressing a finger into her.

She threw her arm across her mouth to stifle her cry of joy, so aroused she could barely stand it.

He stoked her desire with tender ruthlessness, refusing to do more than let a few light touches of his thumb pad stroke her where she ached for pressure most. He switched to her other breast, making her want to beg as he continued to tease with those light thrusts of his finger and the not-quite-there caress.

"Zafir, please," she finally pleaded, fisting her hand in his hair to make him stop.

He dragged her hand from the back of his head

and bit the heel of her palm before he slid even lower and pressed her knees open. Then he gave her what she'd been anticipating, but with his tongue.

It was too much. She pushed her hand beneath her pillow and folded it across her face, releasing her sobs of ecstasy as orgasm took her. It was intense and scandalous and so powerful her eyes dampened with emotion while her body continued to tremor with aftershocks.

How could this be sinful? How?

When he rose over her and stole her pillow, she only thought, *yes*. Whatever he wanted, yes. If he pushed his length into her, she'd welcome him. Revel in his claiming of her.

He rolled her over and brought her hips up, then pinned his steely shaft between her slippery thighs, trapping her knees in place with his own on either side. Covering her the way every other species mated, he slid a hand to where they touched and pressed his shaft against flesh still tingling with postclimax sensitivity. He started to move.

She fisted her hands into her bedroll and held still for his lovemaking, wishing he was inside her. She wanted him to feel the same pleasure he'd given her and—

"Oh!" she gasped as the friction deepened and

caused a sharp sensation to yank her back into arousal.

"Shh," he urged, slowing his movements, caressing her hip and breast. "Are you okay?"

"Yes," she breathed. "Don't stop." She grabbed her pillow and buried her moans into it, giving herself over to him and his needs and the excitement he was rekindling in her. She moved with him, finding the rhythm, wanting this to be the real thing, unable to believe she was almost there again, almost...

They found the crisis together, the sweetness of it so intense she forgot to breath, but maybe that was his arm locked around her rib cage. She kneeled in his fierce grip, loving the feel of his muscles twitching with contractions as she held in her scream of abandonment as her thighs quivered in ecstasy.

His heart continued to pound against her shoulder even after they'd collapsed onto their sides, spooned together. His breaths stirred her hair and he had one warm hand clasped possessively over her breast.

Fern blinked to focus in the dark, stunned by how wild that had been. Very lusty. Kind of dirty. Yet it made her feel so close to him. She resisted the urge to snuggle backward into him, but he stroked his hand down her front and tugged her tight against him, then kissed her shoulder before he relaxed with his nose in her hair.

She blinked her damp eyes, feeling cherished and safe.

"I want to see you. All of you," he whispered.

"Why?" she asked, warming at the thought.

"Because I think your freckles would be pretty."

"They're not. I look like a speckled pony. That's what my mother used to say. She didn't like them. Should you stay?" she asked, partly to change the subject, partly because she wanted to prepare herself. This was really nice, but she had to remember it was temporary. "I don't want to fall asleep."

"Can you put your tablet on vibrate and set the alarm?"

As she reached through the dark to where she'd left it and clicked it on, he tilted the light to her chest.

"Don't," she murmured, lifting it away and tapping, showing him the time she set.

"That's fine," he agreed, gathering her into his naked length as she set it away again. "Why didn't she like them?" He caressed down to her belly and back up to her breast.

"Probably because I got them from my father. Maybe just because they were a part of me. She didn't like me much."

His hand stalled on her hip. "Are you being serious?"

"I shouldn't be, should I? I'll stop." She rolled into him and nuzzled her nose into the hair sprinkled against his breastbone, hands fondling between them. "Why are you still hard? I thought men, you know, relaxed after."

He'd run a towel down her belly and thighs before pulling her to the mattress with him. They'd definitely found their pleasure together.

"I'd dearly love to know how to 'relax' around you, Fern. Being hard this much hurts."

Don't laugh, she thought, pretty sure that men didn't have much of a sense of humor when it came to sexual frustration, but she was insanely flattered.

"I feel the same, like I'm some kind of sex addict, thinking about you all the time. Is it always like this?" she asked, stroking him with a light grip. "I've never felt so greedy about anything. Sometimes I might think, 'oh, that man is handsome,' or something like that, but I've never wanted to—" *Take a man with my mouth.*

She really wanted to do that. He was covering her hand, teaching her how he liked to be stroked. As she found the rhythm, she searched out his flat nipple with her mouth. It was a bold move, but that's what he'd done to her and she'd loved it. Surely he would, too?

He cupped the back of her head, then tilted her up for his kiss. She let him have the lead for a while, but he was so steely and aroused. So intriguing. All she could think about was owning him the way he had taken possession of her.

"I want to do something," she whispered as she pulled away and pressed his shoulder so he was flat on his back.

As she slid down his body, he went hard all over, like he was made of marble. "You don't have to."

"I want to. Tell me how to make it good."

"It's already good."

She laughed. "I'm not there yet."

"I know, but it's still great," he whispered, making her smile as she touched her lips to his hot, velvety shape.

Zafir had one foot in heaven, one in hell.

He counted the daylight hours until he could go to Fern, and cursed when the sun arrived, extinguishing another night with her. When he picked up the message relayed from base camp, his heart sank into the underworld.

He told Ra'id first, because it was expected that he would.

"I have to leave in the morning," Zafir said, explaining the situation with demonstrators in his home city.

"I've been thinking of leaving myself," Ra'id admitted. "Amineh wants to stay the full two weeks, and the girls would live here if I could arrange it, but I'm restless. There are things I should be looking after at home. We've had the meeting we needed. It's time."

Zafir nodded. They were both high-energy men, used to demanding days and schedules that took them around the world in a week. As children they'd been neighbors and acquaintances. At boarding school, they'd gravitated to each other, Ra'id for Zafir's mastery of English and Zafir for Ra'id's understanding and sharing of his Arab blood. As adults they were as close as brothers and never tired of each other's company, but they also knew and respected the responsibilities each had. Idleness was not a natural state for either of them, so leaving made sense.

But Zafir wasn't ready.

"You look genuinely worried. Is this demonstration worse than the others?" Ra'id asked.

"No," Zafir said, consciously clearing his scowl, but unable to stop thinking about what he would be giving up. "It's the same group that rabble-rouses every time I'm away. Things will settle the minute I'm in residence so I'll go home and make that happen." He wouldn't ignore these small uprisings as his father had done, allowing them to escalate into riots and bloodshed.

"This man who keeps causing unrest. Abu

Gadiel? I thought you were going to marry his daughter and quiet him for good?"

Zafir gave a tight smile at the running joke. "That suggestion is looking less outlandish and more practical every day." His mouth twisted on the words. He was not quite ready to face what could be inevitable.

Ra'id snorted, then sobered as he saw the gravity in Zafir's expression. "You're really considering it."

"She's nineteen. Young, educated traditionally, but she's continuing her schooling, planning to be a doctor."

"So she's smart, but perhaps not as interested in playing politics as she is in helping all people," Ra'id suggested.

"Exactly." Not a bad match at all.

"Pretty?"

Zafir cut him a does-it-matter? look.

Ra'id only shrugged. "It hclps."

"I never did give you that herd of goats for taking my ugly sister off my hands," Zafir drawled, making Ra'id's mouth twitch with humor. Ra'id had begun drooling over Amineh before they'd left third form. If he could have, he would have married her before she'd finished school. Their father had been gone by then and it had been up to Zafir to insist his sister pass her A levels before she could marry.

She had, and not only had she been able to marry, but she'd also married for love. Zafir knew she believed he'd come to love Tariq's mother, but it was not an emotion he'd ever aspired to. It had been his father's weakness. The driver of actions that had been his undoing.

Love, for him, was a luxury he couldn't afford. Another arranged marriage for the sake of peace was his lot.

"You'll let me know if there's anything I can do to assist," Ra'id said.

"Appreciated," Zafir said, slapping his friend on the shoulder as he moved away. "I'll let the children know." It was an excuse to see Fern. They did their best to avoid each other during the day, which made him feel a heel, but what option did he have? He'd promised her he wouldn't cost her her job.

"Promise them you'll send Tariq to us for a few weeks. I'll find a pocket in my schedule after my cousin's wedding. It will soften the blow," Ra'id said.

Fine for Tariq and the girls, but how would he soften the blow to himself?

Amineh was sitting in on Fern's lesson today, lending her excellent art skills to sketches of "my favorite animal spotted in the oasis." When Zafir arrived to say everyone would be leaving in the morning, her tiny class erupted into disorder. Amineh was most vocal of all.

"You know I can't ignore these things," Zafir told his sister testily.

Fern was afraid to look at him, certain she'd betray her distress. This was it. The end of her nights with strong arms around her, the scent of a man on her skin, his lips whispering praise and compliments into her soul. It wasn't just the pleasure he gave her that she'd miss, but the illusion of closeness. She was sure he laughed with all the women in his bed, told them all they were pretty and tasted like honey and smelled like wildflowers, but this was her first experience with pillow talk and she loved it.

As he walked away, she couldn't help a yearning look at his back, wishing life wasn't so unfair—

He moved out of sight and her gaze came back to the group and Amineh's alert, probing stare.

The burn of a hard flush swelled up from Fern's throat, choking her and making her cheeks ache. She was such an *idiot*.

Somehow she managed to say, "Didn't you tell me all your friends suffer the effect? He's..." She lifted a helpless, hopeless palm. There weren't words to describe how compelling he was or why she'd fallen under his spell. She just had.

Amineh's shoulders fell and she smiled with

amused sympathy. "They do. And you shouldn't take it personally that he's completely oblivious. Oh, Fern."

Fern waved away the compassion, glad Amineh assumed her crush was platonic, not one fueled by midnight encounters of the most licentious kind. But the prospect of losing those trysts sat like a knife in her chest.

Fortunately the news they were leaving cast a pall over the whole camp. Her long face was one of many. The children were querulous, distracting the adults from Fern's morose mood, and when Tariq invited her to join them for the final meal, she had a valid excuse to maintain her privacy and keep her misery from being noticed.

"I really do have a lot to gather up and pack. I'm sorry."

"I'll miss you," he told her, making her want to hug him, which was odd for her. She had worked with children his age as part of her certification, had enjoyed them immensely, but being affectionate with students wasn't encouraged and she wasn't naturally effusive. Perhaps Zafir had unlocked something in her. She finally felt like she had warmth to offer.

"I'll miss you, too. You're a remarkable young man. But I'll see you in a few months, when you visit your cousins."

She wouldn't see his father, but what she had

with Zafir was already stolen property, not something she could keep.

She took her time memorizing every aspect of him when she held him that night. He seemed to be doing the same. They'd taken to drawing out their caresses these last few nights, letting the sensations build upon themselves, learning to hold each other at the height of passion so every sensation was played out to its greatest degree.

He sat with his back against pillows pushed up against her stack of packed bags and baskets. She kneeled on either side of his thighs, both of them naked and damp, trembling with arousal. Her mouth couldn't stop feasting on his and his hands were firm and thorough, like he intended to imprint his touch on her skin forever.

Rising onto her knees under the urge of his hand on her bottom, she offered her breast for his loving attention. They had perfected silent communication, keeping talking to a minimum for fear of discovery, making love blind in the dark.

He tugged at her nipple, tender and bruised by the sweet, nightly torture of his insatiable appetite. It hurt and felt so good. She let her head fall back as she fought groaning aloud at the acute sensations. How would she survive without him? Without this? She'd never felt so free as she did when she was with him. He was magic and fantasy and perfection.

Folding her arms around his head, she kissed his hair and drank in his dark scent, her eyes burning with an emotion she feared was far deeper and more permanent than infatuation.

He pulled back and drew her down to kiss her hard, to stake his claim on her mouth in a fierce way that threw her heart into flight. She pressed herself to him and writhed in desperation, wanting to crawl inside him and stay with him forever.

Her movements slid her throbbing loins against his rampant erection, so firm and ready. She felt like her hands knew that part of him better than she knew her own body. She moved herself against him, wet and aching, aware that abandoning herself this way aroused him nearly to the breaking point.

The carnality of it thrilled her, made her yearn. Rubbing and sliding against him took her very close to drawing him into her. She slowed, savoring every millimeter of his shape against her sensitive core. Pressure threatened as she found his tip and slid away again. Oh that was wickedly tempting, making her entrance weep with desire, strumming her to unbelievably desperate levels.

Barely realizing what she was doing, she grew more deliberate with her movements, pressing harder, liking the piercing intensity and stretch against her aching center. She did it again, pressing for that hot thickness to sink deeper into her.

"Fern," he gasped as he pulled back, his hands hard on her hips.

"I want it to be you, Zafir," she sobbed in defeat, scraping her nails across his shoulders as she buried her mouth in his neck. Intense sexual hunger nearly shattered her into weeping. "I don't want another man to be my first. I want it to be you."

He was *right there*. Her body needed his so badly.

"I don't want to hurt you." His words were barely audible and he held himself in such tight control, he trembled.

"You won't," she assured him, rocking and catching him into her, feeling him press to the deepest point yet.

His breath rushed out and his arms slid to lock around her.

"Don't stop me," she begged.

"Gently," he said, shaking hands moving up her back to her shoulders. "Go slow—" He bit off a curse as she sank down a little more.

It did hurt. A lot. But she was so aroused it happened easily and she was so happy to feel him filling her. So dazzled by the unique sensation of sitting on his lap this way, nose-to-nose, lips-to-lips, tender flesh burning as she accommodated his thickness, bodies locked in this ancient way.

She smiled as she kissed him and settled fully

onto him, taking all of him, possessing him as much as he possessed her.

He ran his hands over her, nipping at her mouth with tender, inciting kisses as he whispered soft words in Arabic that sounded sweet and grateful and loving.

He played with her breasts, teased her nipples and made her react with a tight clasp around him. Intense excitement shot stars behind her eyelids. She wriggled with ecstasy, discovering the deliciousness grew the more she rocked.

"Careful. You're driving me mad," he said with a hard hand on her hip. "I'm so close I'm going to lose it if you keep doing that."

She ignored him as she arched and writhed, moving with all the skill she'd learned from him. She gloried in grinding herself tight against him, then pulling away until she could feel the tension in his fingers as he urged her not to let his flesh leave hers. Her entire existence narrowed to the place where they joined, where her flesh was taut and sensitized and quivered in joy.

And every time she clasped herself tight on him, a deeper pleasure crept closer, like waves lapping at her, climbing, swelling, threatening to engulf her.

"I'm there, Zafir," she breathed in his ear, feeling the tidal wave rising inside her. "Come with me. It's so good. So good." She sank onto him, clinging as the crisis arrived, expanding a white light through her that was pure elation. Exaltation.

Her body clenched around his shape, stunning her with the intensity of it, the tremendous heightening of their connection. He held her so tightly, she could barely breathe, but she needed his arms to hold her together as she shook and her abdomen contracted in ecstatic catches of bliss.

In the middle of it all, she fell, flying, plummeting and landing on her back on a bed of silken sheets. His big body covered hers and his hips moved in sharp, possessive thrusts, stinging her tight flesh, but escalating her orgasm into a new realm. He muffled her cries of joy with a hard kiss and bucked, filling her as his body convulsed in release.

She locked her knees at his waist, embracing him. Her ankles hooked in the small of his back, trying to keep him in her forever.

And when his weight settled fully onto her, she let her breath release with gratitude, utterly at peace. Happier than she'd ever been in her life.

In love, hopelessly and irrevocably in love, but that's how a woman should feel with her first, right?

Zafir forced himself to gather his strength and roll away.

Leaving Fern was like stripping his body from

his soul, but that part of him would be consigned to hell for this anyway.

It was as dark in her tent as it was every night that he stole in here, but he threw his arm over his eyes anyway, trying to block out reality.

He had meant to pull out.

He had never intended to fully possess her at all, but she'd tempted him beyond bearing, her desire for him the juiciest forbidden fruit to a man going mad with thirst.

And she'd been exquisite. Despite his best efforts to retain his sanity, he'd lost himself to the moment. To her erotic movements. Her heat and the pound of her heart against his own and the fire raging in his blood.

He didn't even remember how she'd wound up under him, had only come back to real awareness of where he was and how wrong this was when the crisis had been peaked. The most all-encompassing satisfaction had filled him.

Until awareness had crept in with the slowing of his heart rate. Her tight, wet fit around him. Her soft sigh of repletion.

This should *not* have happened.

"Zafir—" she began in a whisper.

"Shh." He came up on his elbow and touched her lips with his finger, listening.

Across the camp, he heard one of the girls sobbing and Amineh's comforting voice going to her.

The small action of caressing Fern's tender mouth and catching her scent rising warmly off her body made him stir with renewed excitement. He couldn't trust himself if he stayed here. He'd have her again and now they weren't the only ones awake in the camp.

"I have to go," he whispered as he leaned close. "Before we're caught."

Her lips tightened under his touch in a flinch. "Okay."

Her acceptance of his loving and leaving made him disgusted with himself. He wanted to ask about timing, but if he stayed any longer, he'd kiss her, fist his hand in her hair and make love to her all over again. Letting her go and rising from her bed was the hardest thing he'd ever done, but he made himself do it. He left her without saying goodbye, because he was afraid he'd fail to do it at all if he didn't do it fast and quiet.

Later that morning, he ensured his caravan was ready first. He hugged his sister and kissed his nieces and learned from their father that Jumanah had been crying in the night because she didn't want to leave.

He could relate.

He wouldn't let himself dwell on the silky hold of Fern's body, though, or the clinging limbs that had clawed with passion for his.

"Goodbye, Miss Davenport," he managed to

say when Fern brought one of her bags to the camel keepers. He wanted to ask where she was in her cycle, but they weren't alone.

She wore sunglasses and her mouth pouted sexily—from sadness? Or his insatiable kisses last night?

"Thank you, abu Tariq," she said. Their use of more formal names reset their relationship to where it ought to be. Her pale face colored with a pretty shade of pink as she added, "For making it possible for me to visit such a remarkable place." Her voice wavered and color came up in her cheeks like a thermometer in the sun.

His heart twisted. It had been extraordinary for him, too.

"Bissalama" was all he said. *Have a safe journey.* It made him feel small until she replied in her quiet voice.

"You, too. Always."

He took a breath that he wished could knock the weight off his heart, nodded and moved to take the reins of his camel.

CHAPTER SIX

FERN MIGHT HAVE pined away her life if she hadn't been so distracted, but within a few weeks of returning to the palace, the entire family was packed up to attend a wedding of Ra'id's cousin in the south.

Ra'id's country was quite conservative, but this new state was even more so. Fern had to relinquish her passport at the airport and was given a room in a modern-day harem. The annexed compound was a collection of bungalows around a courtyard with an opulent pool, fountains and bronze statues. One passageway led to the main palace.

Her rooms were very nice, but few people bothered to speak to her—just the other foreigners, one a Malaysian nanny and another the wife of a pastry chef flown in from Paris. The rest of the women were family from both sides of the wedding party and came and went, keeping to themselves.

Fern didn't mind. She was slipping quietly into

a state of terror as she awaited proof she and Zafir hadn't cashed in on the gamble they'd taken that last night. Unfortunately, her cycle grew later by the hour, making her certain they had.

Impossible, she thought. They'd only made love the once. Loads of women took years of active trying to get pregnant. How could she wind up pregnant after one time?

She wrung her hands as she waited for Amineh to collect the girls one afternoon. The girls had another dress-fitting today, but Amineh was adamant that they keep as much to routine as possible. Jumanah was mixing up the direction of her letters, which wasn't uncommon at this age, but Amineh wanted Fern to stay on top of it to ensure it wasn't a more serious concern.

"I kept putting off starting Bashira's schooling because we had so many other commitments and now she's six and will fall behind her peers if I don't make their education a priority," Amineh had said when asking Fern to accompany them on this trip. "I know it won't be ideal, but will you come?"

Fern hadn't been able to say no. Teaching the girls was what she was contracted to do. Plus, she enjoyed the distraction of learning every nuance and aspect of this culture she was immersed in. Welcomed it.

Her mind kept screaming, *it was* one *time*.

Completely the wrong time in her cycle, too. She didn't understand it.

But what was there to understand? Sex made babies. She had had sex.

She and Zafir had made—

No.

But as the days wore on and the tenderness in her breasts became nearly unbearable and her churning stomach couldn't be blamed solely on worry, she accepted that she was as bad as—quite possibly worse than—her mother. Fern, at least, had had the benefit of her mother's lectures. She should have *known* better.

The final straw was a pronouncement by Amineh. When she arrived for the girls, she looked as washed out as Fern felt. The girls ran to their quarters to change while Amineh huffed out an exhausted breath.

"Ra'id told me Zafir was talking about arranging another marriage for himself, to the daughter of one of his challengers. Brilliant, I said. I want peace in Q'Amara as much as he does, but if he thinks I'm putting myself through another wedding before this baby comes out— Oh, I've shocked you." Amineh's hand came onto her arm. "I thought you might have guessed after I nearly fainted on you this morning. You sounded so sympathetic, like you knew what I was going through in this heat."

"Oh, no, I—" Fern was dumbfounded. Part of her went into cardiac arrest at what else she might have betrayed by being "sympathetic," the rest was screaming in agony at what Amineh had just told her. She did her best to shake it all off. "No, I honestly didn't realize," she said. She'd been too obsessed with the possibility she was pregnant herself. "That's wonderful. Congratulations."

She hugged Amineh and couldn't help the tears that came into her eyes. Expecting with her friend was so perfect, yet such a disaster.

"Oh, Fern, you really are the sweetest person, crying for me. Honestly, I feel like crying myself. I'm so tired, and look! Barely six weeks and I feel like I'm beginning to show. Nothing fits right. Ra'id is being a gem, making my excuses and promising me that after this, we're home for a year, but we have another two *weeks* of this nonsense."

Fern could only offer a shaky smile, wishing the father of *her* baby would be a gem and look after *her*, but he had an entire country to worry about.

And he was getting married.

That night she cried until her throat burned and woke to such a violent bout of morning sickness, she knew she could be found out. As much as she wanted to tell Zafir, she couldn't. Not like this, from a country where her condition, especially as an unmarried woman, could be seen as a crime. What if someone found out? What if he didn't care?

Staring at her ravaged face the next morning, she knew what she had to do. She was a terrible liar, but at least her emotions were on such a seesaw, her anxiety so very real, that when she requested a meeting with Ra'id, she looked convincingly distraught.

"I've had some bad news from home. A dear friend. She's like a mother to me." Miss Ivy was perfectly fine, as far as Fern knew, but as Fern considered the way she'd derailed this wonderful career she'd been given, fresh tears came into her eyes. "I'm so sorry. I need to return to England immediately."

Amineh was out with the girls and other women from the wedding party. Fern had planned it that way, unable to speak her bald-faced lies directly to someone she considered a true friend. Especially when she'd betrayed that friendship by sleeping with Amineh's brother.

It was far easier to let Ra'id recoil from her display of feminine emotions, snap into making arrangements and put her on a plane within the hour. She promised she would be in touch about her return, claiming it shouldn't be more than a week or two.

Her first order of business after checking in to

her London hotel half a day later was a pregnancy test. Her life changed completely in the one minute it took to watch the blue positive sign appear. She had known, but now she *knew*.

Sitting on the edge of the bathtub, she saw her dream job dissolve into a blur, just like her pale reflection in the mirror across from her. She couldn't face Amineh after this. Couldn't face Zafir after being so stupid as to let it happen. She couldn't put him in a position of choosing between his country and her. Not when she knew something of the anguish he and his sister had grown up in, feeling torn between two worlds. She couldn't do that to her child.

She was having a baby!

Unable to process that reality, she went through the motions of what had to be done. She wrote her resignation letter with hands that shook so badly she could barely type. Then she made arrangements for the agency to forward it on her behalf. Her apologies were profuse, her regret profound, but she was unable to return. The circumstances here at home made it impossible, she said, and wished the girls well in their studies.

After cutting those final ties, the day after her arrival in London, she put herself on a train to the north and took a cab from the station to Miss Ivy's flat.

"Fern!" her friend gasped when she opened the door. "I wasn't expecting you!"

Fern dropped her cases. "I am. Expecting." Now came the tears as the magnitude of it all finally hit her. "Oh, Miss Ivy! What am I going to *do*?"

Six months later

Zafir was preparing for a very private, very delicate meeting. Abu Gadiel had agreed to let Zafir introduce himself to his daughter. They, with her mother and two brothers, were arriving at any minute. The air in his expansive office was already thick with tension and he was the only one in it.

Zafir silently went over his reasons for seeking a union with her, how it would strengthen confidence in his ruling of the country while giving her father a voice near his ear. It would benefit the country they all cared about. He already knew her only reservation: whether she would be allowed to continue her ambitions to become a doctor.

He would encourage her, of course. Offer a long engagement, wait until she'd finished her degree even. It would press him into celibacy, but he would need time to work up the desire to bed her anyway. Sexual hunger tortured him every hour of every day, but he only thought of one woman.

This obsession had to stop. He would *not* become his father, keeping a mistress in England. That way led to the madness of falling in love, having a family as though they were a proper couple with a future. Q'Amara needed stability. That came from a man with a clear mind, not one tortured by passionate emotions like love.

So he would ignore the fact that Fern had gone back to England, even though the knowledge had sent a rush of excitement roaring through him. The imperative to go and stamp and ensconce had been pacing like an angry lion inside him since Tariq had come home with the news of her departure from Ra'id's palace. A widowed Mrs. Heath was in residence as Fern's replacement. She was nice enough, but didn't make jokes or let them wander off topic. Photos had shown a woman of later years, white hair and a plump body.

"Why did she leave?" Zafir had questioned Tariq, experiencing a pierce that should have been fear, but was too anticipatory.

"Her friend was sick. Auntie said it sounded like what my mother had."

Zafir's mind had sheared off the thought that had barely formed, that Fern had had another reason for leaving, and he'd focused on reminding Tariq that rules were relaxed at the oasis. *An understatement.* Miss Davenport might also have been strict if she'd been in her proper classroom, he'd said, so Tariq shouldn't be too hard on the new Mrs. Heath.

Tariq hadn't agreed, insisting Miss Davenport was superior in every way, but they'd moved on to other things.

And Zafir had spent weeks imagining where he would buy her a flat in London, even going so far as to look at real estate listings. He didn't even know what she might like. They hadn't talked much, always too busy quietly eating each other alive. Obviously she'd always lived modestly. He'd gathered that she'd taken care of her mother through a terminal illness. Surely she would appreciate not having to work or worry about meeting her basic needs anymore.

His desire to continue their affair was a type of insanity. An obsession. It had to stop. He tilted his head back, fighting yet again the memory of having her under him, lissome and smelling like heaven, hot and writhing with abandon. Had he known he *would* have her, he would have taken her from the beginning. All the way, every night.

The knock on his door was like an axe hitting the chopping block. No more thoughts of her after today. His life was moving in a different direction. A necessary one.

But when he called permission to enter, his guest was Ra'id.

Zafir frowned. His brother-in-law never arrived unannounced and never looked so grim. Zafir's mind instantly whirled into terrible possibilities. He rejected each frightening concern as quickly as it came. Please not his sweet nieces. Let Amineh be well. She was pregnant. Was something wrong with the baby?

"What's happened?" he demanded as Ra'id closed the door behind himself.

Ra'id lifted a staying hand. "Your sister and the children are fine. But she has insisted I come see you, since she's too far along to travel and confront you herself."

Ra'id looked more severe than Zafir had ever seen him, as if an angry black cloud surrounded him. The accusation narrowing his friend's eyes suggested he pinned some sort of blame on Zafir.

That took him aback. He tried to think of what Tariq might have possibly done during his stay three months ago. He'd talked of one of Ra'id's prized horses...

Folding his arms, Ra'id stated belligerently, "My wife and I have been arguing for months. I knew she was keeping something from me, which is not like her at all." The couched fury in Ra'id's voice put Zafir on high alert. "And when she finally told me her suspicions, I assured her she was so wrong that this would go down in our marriage as the most unfounded disagreement we have ever had."

"She cannot be accusing you of an affair?" Zafir said with disbelief. His friend had been married to Amineh long before the formal ceremony had taken place. If Ra'id had had any other lover but his wife, Zafir would be shocked dead.

"Not me, no," Ra'id said, adopting the full superiority of his station. "You."

Zafir's breath stalled. His lifetime of being attacked with denigrations served him well. He deflected this one with a neutral expression and only elevated one eyebrow as he blithely responded, "I'm not married."

"Miss Davenport left our household rather abruptly some months ago. Amineh is convinced you are the reason."

"This *will* go down in history as a ridiculous fight if you've come all this way to involve me in your domestic employment issues," Zafir intoned.

"It has turned into a contest of which one of us knows you better. She thinks you quite capable of an affair with her friend, while I have assured her you have more honor and sense."

And so they were found out. Zafir's ears rang as he met his friend's eyes. It wasn't comfortable to let Ra'id see that he would not go home crowing about being right. Zafir did, indeed, have less honor and sense than his best friend had credited him.

Ra'id's face tightened. "Because it was obvious to anyone with eyes that Miss Davenport was not the type to engage in affairs, I said. As much of a hound that your brother can be, he indulges himself elsewhere with sophisticated women who know what they're getting into. The kind who accept jewelry, but don't expect a diamond ring. He would never prey on a virgin dormouse and take advantage of her."

Self-disgust rose like a cloud of grit inside Zafir. He couldn't hide it.

"You had an affair with my children's teacher," Ra'id persisted as Zafir failed to deny the implications. Ra'id's voice rose with genuine fury. "Do you realize they have just now stopped crying for her? She was under my protection, Zafir!"

"You slept with my sister before you married her. In my *house*," he snarled back.

"I wanted to marry her," Ra'id retorted. "I *loved* her."

And there was the slap of truth that made Zafir look away. He had told himself Fern was English. English girls had affairs. His actions weren't that dishonorable. *She had wanted it to be him.*

"It was not my best hour," he acknowledged. "I'll admit that." But he wouldn't try to explain it. There was no explaining it. Sexual infatuation had got the better of him. He couldn't offer excuses because there were none.

"So Amineh's intuition strikes where my conviction, my certainty that I knew you better, fails."

"Yes," Zafir said with a tight smile. "I'm sorry that you must now go home and tell your wife you were wrong. A fate worse than death for any man. Are we finished? Because that tap on the door means my guests have arrived."

"No," Ra'id said with false pleasantry. "Because if she's right about your sleeping with her, she might be right about something else. You see, the piece that has been really bothering her is the way Miss Davenport has cut off all communication."

For a moment that made Zafir wonder. Worry. Was she ill? Then he remembered… "She's nursing a sick friend. People insulate themselves in that situation." He had, when his wife had been dying. You tired of singing the sad song, giving details that were the furthest thing from optimistic, looking into pitying eyes and facing the inevitability of your own mortality.

"Is she?" Ra'id asked, tucking his hands behind his back and rocking onto his heels. The edges of his *gutra* swayed around his supercilious expression. "I certainly thought that's why she was leaving, when she came to me so distressed I couldn't put her on an airplane fast enough. But Amineh has tracked this friend online and there's no indication she's suffering anything but impatience with a wet winter. Miss Davenport has let her own accounts go stale while her friend is cheerfully stating that she has begun a training regime for a half marathon and recently posted photos of her mountain trek in Portugal."

Zafir didn't know what to make of that, but he sensed the walls closing in on him.

"Miss Davenport appears to have lied to Amineh. Why would she do that, Zafir? What possible reason could she have to leave so abruptly and fail to return any of Amineh's emails? Shall I tell you the theory your sister, the amateur detective, has formulated?"

Please don't. But they both knew what the most logical conclusion was.

"She would have told me," Zafir muttered as a refutation, wanting to believe it. Because the alternative, that Fern was pregnant with his child and hadn't told him, was too much to face. The reasons behind choosing *not* to tell him were too ugly to absorb.

"Another type of woman would have tried to trap you," Ra'id said. "She would have told you and extorted a lifetime of support. Marriage even. Did this woman even have the sense to use birth control? Did *you*?"

Zafir's skin was dark enough to be Arab, but his green eyes were windows into his impure soul. All of him burned in the fire of culpability as he

stood there, a man as close as a brother judging
him for his reprehensible behavior. He had abandoned any sense of consequence. He was no better than the father who had condemned him to
this half life of never belonging.

He had no defense for his actions.

"Ya gazma," Ra'id spat. *You shoe.* Zafir felt
lower than a shoe.

"She would have told me," Zafir insisted. Had
she been too embarrassed? Or was it shame?

"She quit because she feared running into you
again?" Ra'id queried. "Given how sensitive and
conscientious she seemed, I could believe that.
But you better find out if that's all it was before
you proceed with what you've started here." Ra'id
jerked his chin toward the door and the place
where Zafir's proposed fiancée waited.

Zafir's heart sank like a stone in quicksand,
slow and inevitable and irretrievable. He had ru-
ined everything. He was a disgrace.

He ran a hand down his burning face, trying
to think.

"What will you do if she's pregnant?" There
was the voice of his friend. Anger had abated
and troubled understanding clouded Ra'id's eyes.
He knew what a terrible position Zafir could be
in.

Somehow this reaction was worse. Zafir would
rather be reviled than consoled.

Why had he allowed something so superficial to go so far? Was it in his blood to be this careless?

He shut down the rage of helplessness. It was done. He had to find out if Fern was pregnant.

"I don't know," he responded truthfully, voice as bleak as the rest of him.

"I had time to think on the way here," Ra'id said. "I have a suggestion."

CHAPTER SEVEN

FERN HURRIED FROM the bus stop with the collar of her raincoat clutched tightly closed against her throat. With her other hand, she grasped the umbrella in a firm grip against the midday gusts trying to yank it away. The rushed walk made her breathless, partly due to the extra weight, she supposed. Possibly because she needed more iron.

Pregnancy was a lot of work, she had discovered with a small pang of understanding for her mother's beleaguered outlook. It was disconcerting to feel as though your body wasn't yours anymore, but she didn't resent the process, *Mother*. She didn't blame this baby growing inside her for the anxiety she felt about their future.

She blamed herself.

Tramping quickly through the puddles in her boots, she felt icy splashes strike her knees through her tights, urging her even faster toward the sanctuary of Miss Ivy's little flat. Not a whole house. Not even a proper two-bedroom. Fern was on the sofa bed at Miss Ivy's insistence, saving the nest egg she had squirrelled away during her teaching contract with Amineh. She was even bringing in a few extra pounds with some adult tutoring. She hoped to take over a flat two blocks away when it came available in a few months.

None of this was ideal. In fact, it was the kind of repetition of history she hated to own up to, but she would manage. And her baby would not carry the burden of fault that had been hers most of her life.

As she reached the steps to the converted row house that held Miss Ivy's flat, the self-satisfied lambent green town car at the curb caught her attention. Its tinted windows and details of chrome where out of place in this village. The driver's side door opened, startling her into halting.

Zafir straightened and slammed the door with a firmness that made her flinch. As he came around the bonnet, seemingly unaware of the rain that pattered onto his uncovered head, she told herself to run, but could only stand there and stare.

No tunic or headdress, but he was as exotic and resplendent as always, even in a bespoke English suit of cast-iron-gray with a sharp white shirt and a silver tie. His beard was shaved to a narrow line that edged his set jaw and cut a goatee around the uncompromising firmness of his mouth.

His remarkable green eyes were as flat as

frosted glass as they traveled to the billow of her overcoat. He flinched, but it wasn't with surprise. More like, *okay then*.

The way he moved was smooth and unhurried, but his approach still felt like a blast of hurricane-force wind. He covered her hand on the umbrella and lifted it high enough so he could stand under it with her. Her hearing dulled and became more acute at the same time. Damp, earthy, male scents of aftershave and coffee, wool and warm, masculine skin, clouded into the little space and overwhelmed her senses.

She swallowed, falling into lust all over again.

Pathetic. She was in the middle of her third trimester, about as sexy as a cow ready to calf, but she wanted to lie with him. Naked and joined.

"Let's get out of this mess," he said in the voice that had been raising the hairs on her scalp since the first time she'd heard it.

Out of the rain? Or the situation?

Her heart kicked into gear as he nudged her into movement. His free hand grazed her elbow and he pointed her in the direction of the steps. She began to tremble as the enormity of his being here hit.

Did he know? Of course he did *now*. She wasn't the size of a house, but her coat was tented over her bump like a tarp over the bow of a boat. That radiation of umbrage from him was unmistakable.

She'd grown up with those sorts of vibes directed at her. She knew all too well this sense of disapproval jabbing into her like the point of a sword.

But had he known? Had he come to see her? Or because he'd learned of the baby? How?

As they stepped into the small space beneath the overhang of the stoop, he stole the umbrella from her nerveless grip, lowered and shook it, then followed her through the door that her numb fingers could barely unlock. He dropped the umbrella into its stand and paced his footsteps into hers as they climbed the two narrow flights to Miss Ivy's door.

Her mind raced, but she couldn't seem to catch a solid thought. Bring him into the flat? Take him somewhere else? Where? Why was he here? What was he going to say?

How much did he hate her for this?

"Fern?" Miss Ivy called from the tiny alcove of the kitchen as they entered. "A woman called for you. She didn't leave her name, but I told her you'd be back about now so I expect—"

Miss Ivy trailed off as she emerged with a glass and a tea towel in hand. "Hello," she said with a lilt of curiosity in her tone, eyes going sharp as she looked into Fern's face—which had to be ghostly pale. Her brows pulled together with concern.

"That was my assistant," Zafir explained. "You

must be Ivy McGill? Thank you for saving me the trouble of waiting in the rain any longer than I had to. You're well? Our family was given to understand you were quite ill."

His tone dripped sarcasm. Fern tried to ignore it.

"Miss Ivy, this is Sheikh abu Tariq Zafir ibn Ahmad al-Rakin Iram. Or you might be more familiar with him as, um, Mr. Zafir Cavendish, grandson of the Duke of Sommerton, who sits in the House of Lords. I did—" she cleared her throat "—give the impression that you were in need of care when I cut short my teaching contract with his sister's children."

"I see." No doubt Miss Ivy saw very well. No one had ever accused her of lacking math skills.

"Let me take your coat, Fern," Zafir said, stepping behind her so her heart nearly leaped out her mouth.

You don't live here. It's not your job to take my coat, she wanted to protest. *Don't stay. Don't talk to me. Don't even look at me.*

Then she felt the brush of his fingertips against her shoulders and the sensuous memory of his stripping her clothing from her body came back to her like sunshine breaking its warmth across her face. She suppressed a shiver of mixed longing and mortification.

He stepped away to hang the dripping coat on

the hooks over the rubber mat. Fern balanced a hand on the wall and unzipped her boots, taking extraordinary care with placing them so the insides wouldn't be filled by the rivulets off her coat, afraid to turn and face him.

"Why don't you make us some tea," Zafir suggested behind her, but Fern suspected he was looking at her, not Miss Ivy. He was willing her to face him and own up to what she'd done. "Fern and I need to talk."

Hugging herself, as if that could disguise this huge evidence of her carelessness that stretched the knit of her oversized jumper, Fern forced herself around.

Miss Ivy looked worried. She had pressed Fern many times to tell her who the father was and now there was such anxiety in her small dark eyes.

Fern managed a tight smile. "It's fine," she assured her.

Miss Ivy nodded jerkily and slipped into the alcove, where she'd be able to hear the murmur of their voices while she filled the kettle and brought out her good china.

Fern dared a glance at Zafir and saw a puzzling mixture of emotions on his face. He aimed his hard stare at her belly. Something fierce yet angry gripped him. Not dangerously threatening, but deeply primal.

She swallowed and edged toward the sofa,

where she lowered to perch on the edge of the cushion, facing him, facing up to all of this that she'd mostly been denying. Visiting a doctor and reading ads for flats was only the tip of the iceberg as far as fully accepting her pregnancy went.

A rush of despondency hit as the biggest part that she'd been avoiding—the fact her baby had a father—confronted her with ominous silence.

"I didn't mean for this to happen, Zafir." Her voice was husky with self-castigation.

"It's mine," he said, more statement than question, but the demand for confirmation made her choke out a shocked laugh.

"Who else?" she asked, askance.

"I needed to hear it." He looked away, his profile carved sharply from granite. His hand fisted at his side and his jaw worked, but the news didn't seem to please him.

"Are you surprised?" she asked as she realized how much easier it would be for him if she'd been promiscuous. And even as her mind told her to change her answer—make things easy so maybe he wouldn't hate her—she blurted, "Sorry I'm not a slut with a list of possible fathers—"

He swung his gaze back. The hardness in his aqua eyes buttoned her lip.

She felt enough of a slut as it was, whether he wanted to call her one or not. She clenched her pale fingers together, rather wishing for the warmth of a blush to take away this bone-deep chill.

"Why didn't you tell me?" he asked, his tone so tight with fury she flinched.

"I didn't think you would want to know," she answered, hating how thin her voice had gone.

Again with the glare that encased her in ice.

"Was there something in the way I treat Tariq that suggested to you I would take no interest in my child?"

"No." She bowed her head under his stark condemnation. His relationship with his son had actually tempted her to tell him, *But I didn't want you to think I did this on purpose. We both know this is...* She couldn't bring herself to call her baby a mistake, but the situation was far from ideal. "You're not happy, Zafir. You're barely holding on to a civil tone." She squirmed her fingers together. "It seemed better not to tell you."

"And do what instead?"

"What do you mean?"

"Are you keeping it?"

"Obviously." She waved at the size of her belly.

"I mean, are you thinking to give it up for adoption or something?"

"No!" The suggestion astonished her, never once occurring to her as a realistic possibility.

He looked away again, not giving her a chance to read his eyes, but some of his animosity seemed to ease as he said with a husk of emotion, "So you want this baby."

"Yes! Why would you imagine anything else?"

"You tried to keep my child out of my life, Fern. It follows that you might want to purge it from your own." He swung his attention back to her and the force of his gaze kicked her low and hard.

Maybe that was the baby, scolding her. She had worried, for about ten minutes, that she would begrudge her child for coming along when she'd finally been free of family obligation. But it wasn't as if she had had high career plans or wanted to live fast. While her mother had felt cheated as a single parent and had made sure to let Fern know it, Fern viewed raising a child alone as a challenge, yes, but a fairly common one. Many women managed this. Yes, she worried about her future, but because her baby would depend on her. Taking care of another life was a responsibility she wanted to get right. She didn't want to mess it up.

But while she'd glossed very quickly past any thoughts of not keeping the baby, Zafir had obviously convinced himself she wouldn't.

"I knew almost from the moment I realized I was pregnant that I'd keep it," she told him quietly. "But when I looked at all the factors…" She frowned at her twisting fingers, still unable to bring all the dangling threads together into anything less than a messy, painful knot. "It seemed like putting you in this position of acknowledging your child was more unfair than keeping you ignorant of it."

"You were offering me plausible deniability? How kind." His voice peeled a layer off her, astringent as paint thinner.

She jerked her gaze up, not liking the acerbic response when she'd honestly been trying to put his needs ahead of her own. "I won't pretend to be an expert on your country's politics, but I know this is the last thing you need. I'm doing what I can to keep the baby secret—"

"Obviously," he said with a bite. "But I'm not here to pay you off. I'm here to claim my child. I want him or her in my life."

Her heart shook in her chest, quaking with both intimidation and the ferocity of a mother whose child was threatened. "Did you miss what I just said? I have no intention of giving it up. Not even to its own father!"

"Then you'll marry me," he stated, like it was as easy as snapping fingers.

And her nerves twanged, mind skewing in a thousand directions because in all her scenarios of what could possibly happen if he learned of this baby, none of them had included his proposing. Even as coldly and flatly as that.

"I…" Her heart, already taxed with stress and

emotion, pounded extra hard. The feeling was nearly painful, making tears spring to her eyes. Live the rest of her life under that baleful glare? After the first twenty years of her life had been blistered by the same? No thanks. "I can't. Or do you mean just to make it legitimate? And I'd stay in England while you—"

"No," he interrupted, adamant. "You'd live with me and Tariq, in our palace."

Which sounded like a fairy tale except for the part where she'd be treated like a troll.

She realized she was biting her lips together and forced them to relax, soothing them with her tongue. But he made her so nervous, standing there like a—well, like a damned sultan who could demand she give him a baby. She'd seen this uncompromising side of him at the oasis, when he'd taken control and insisted on treatment for the Bedouin girl. It wasn't a level of command she wanted to pit herself against.

Especially not when he was demanding to be part of his child's life. Her own father hadn't even bothered sticking around to find out if she was a boy or a girl. There was a huge part of her that melted beneath Zafir's show of fatherly interest.

But what about her?

Now she began to understand her mother's sense of lost entitlement. Sure her baby would force her to make certain compromises, but for the most part, alone as a single parent, she controlled their fate. With Zafir in the picture, she faced huge concessions.

See, Mum? You were actually lucky not to have this dilemma.

"Marriage isn't on my radar," she murmured.

"Put it there."

She shook her head.

"Why the hell not?"

Had he listened when she had introduced him? "Think about who you are—"

His head snapped back like she'd struck him.

"That wasn't—" *What she'd meant...*

Miss Ivy clattered her tray into the room, killing Fern's chance to explain.

A hoar frost coated the room as Miss Ivy set everything out and poured. Into the condemning silence, she said, "Shall I take mine into my room?"

"Please," Fern said through a tight throat. She needed privacy to straighten out Zafir's wrong impression.

Fern's roommate was the homeliest woman Zafir had ever seen. Small and hunched, she had dull brown hair streaked in gray, definitely a home cut, teeth like an old cemetery and beady brown eyes that were deeply set.

But as she left, she touched Fern's shoulder with a maternal hand. Fern covered the woman's gnarled knuckles and the glance the two exchanged was complex. Sheepish and forgiving and reassuring. The kind of unspoken communication women had when they were very close.

As one of the two doors off the main room closed, Zafir swung his gaze around the flat. It was charming, he supposed, in the way of modest, dated rooms kept tidy and warm. There was an odd collection of photos showing young men and women in graduation caps and gowns, accepting awards, waving from the window of a pilot's seat and standing at a podium.

"Who is she?" he asked, still reeling from Fern's gross insult, not ready to deal with how deeply she had cut him.

"A teacher. She made me a member of her Shyness Club when I was nine." Her freckled face tinted. "Zafir, that's not what I meant. About you being who you are..."

Her voice trailed off as she twisted her fingers. It would be a wonder if the digits remained attached at the rate she was torturing them.

He wouldn't ask what she *had* meant. Wouldn't wheedle to understand. He didn't even want to face her, there was such an agony of rejection coursing through him, but his gaze snagged on the bump of their child swelling her middle. It continued to stun him. His wife had kept to herself in hundreds of ways, including an almost complete retreat when she became heavily pregnant. If she had been in his presence, she had draped herself in oversized garments that hadn't really let him see evidence of the child she was giving him.

The heir she had hidden like something unwanted and merely endured because her husband was something unwanted and endured. Lower than her. Not good enough.

Still deeply scarred by that disdain, he focused instead on the way Fern let her bump sit so prominently in her lap. He itched to set his hands on her. All of her. She was fuller everywhere, from her cheeks to her breasts to her bottom. It suited her.

Her hair was longer, drying and starting to spring out from its catch at the back of her neck. Her skin was as much a display of cinnamon and cream as ever. She was tempting and as sweet as almonds and honey, he'd thought when he'd stood under the umbrella with her outside. Her scent had mingled with the rain and wind of English storms and struck him as oddly familiar. Heartening.

Everything about her was the same and more, especially her ability to enthrall him.

But she hadn't told him about the baby because of who he was. Didn't she mean *what* he was?

Funny how dozens of women had overlooked his birth and half-caste status, wishing to marry his money and blue blood, but the two females he'd actually proposed to had been unable to get past it.

Misery lined Fern's expression. "I meant that a man in your position could have anyone." Her bottom lip disappeared as she pulled it between her teeth, while her brows crooked and trembled.

"Anyone except you," he challenged, fighting the tightness that gripped him.

Couched hope glimmered in the gray depths of her gaze, but dimmed as he returned her look with one that refused to give anything away.

Obviously struggling to hold on to her composure, she looked away, her voice scraped raw. "You didn't come here for me."

"No," he agreed, aware it was cruel to be so bald, but what did she expect? Declarations of love? They'd had an affair. That was all. He still couldn't believe how many times he'd thought about her. How he'd wanted to set her up in London.

But as he watched her flinch and nod, absorbing his slight, he realized that the woman who had welcomed him each night to her tent was not the sophisticated mistress he had let her become in his mind. The one confident in her allure and ability to drive him mad. No, Fern didn't seem to have any idea the hold she still had on him. The depth of want he felt even more intensely now, when she was within reach. His desire, his ability to rationalize making her his, was greater than ever.

And she made no effort to draw him back. The slump of her shoulders spoke of hopelessness.

He supposed her ignorance was a relief, but it seemed to open a huge gap in the small room, one he didn't know how to bridge.

"How is Amineh?" she asked.

The sudden change of topic threw him.

"Fine," he replied. "According to Ra'id. That was a few days ago. You?" he asked, as it belatedly occurred to him. "Everything is normal with the baby?"

She gave an absent nod. "The supplements make me feel a bit off and I can't stand the smell of sausage or bacon, but we're both healthy and fat." Her doll's mouth pursed in a self-deprecating smile. "That's what the midwife said."

"When are you due?"

She told him.

It was strange to imagine himself a father again and so soon, but as he mentally counted down the handful of weeks, a rush of eagerness to get there and see his son or daughter unexpectedly slid through him. A girl? With kinky red hair and a pert little mouth like her mother? What would Tariq think?

He skimmed a hand over his damp hair. He hadn't even told his son, being totally focused on confronting Fern and discovering if there was a baby on the way. The minute he'd seen her, he'd needed to know it was his. Had needed to claim it.

He wanted to claim her, lies to the contrary and discomfort with the truth notwithstanding. His mind was exploding with the simplicity of it. Of course he would marry her and bring her back to Q'Amara. His personal ethics would accept nothing else.

But she didn't want to marry him. She wasn't looking at him and he couldn't look away from her. Heat climbed in him, some of it embarrassment at his partiality for her, so wrong for him, but a fresh emotion brimmed inside him as he took in her fertile figure: determination. She *would* marry him. She *would* live in his house with his child. They *would* make this work.

He hoped they could make it work. A stealthy fear snaked through him that he was repeating history on more than one front, but he would not turn his back on his child.

"Fern, marriage is the only—"

"No it's not," interrupted. "*You* know it's not."

"I won't be my father," he insisted, growing annoyed as she vehemently shook her head. "This baby might not be heir and successor to Q'Amara, but I won't have an illegitimate child. People would look at Tariq as my 'real' son and say this one is something less. No. We *must* marry."

"You'll hate me," she stated. Then, with the quiet ferocity she'd used when demanding medical attention for the Bedouin girl, she added, "I won't live like that again. I *won't*."

Anguish tortured her expression before she looked away, tears standing on her wide, unblinking eyes. She set her jaw, though, so obviously ready to hold her ground, he had to take her seriously.

"Again?" he prompted, disbelief scuffing his tone. Aside from this current streak of obstinacy, she was fairly compliant. Not someone difficult to get along with. He was furious with her, but couldn't imagine anyone actively disliking her. "What do you mean by that? Who else hated you?"

"My mother," she said in a small voice, looking at her wringing hands. Her pale brows crushed together and the corners of her mouth went down. Bright red lit her cheekbones while the rest of her was so pale her freckles stood out like stress cracks that warned she was on the brink of crumbling. "She got pregnant with me when she was seventeen. Her parents threw her out. My father disappeared. She barely scraped by trying to support me."

"And she blamed you for that?" His heart took a sharp swerve. He distantly remembered her saying something like *she didn't like me much*. He'd been distracted with making love to her, but now the hackles of his parenting instincts rose at the idea of a mother denigrating her child. His own had made a ton of mistakes, but nothing like that.

"She blamed me for all of it," Fern said with equal parts incredulity and despondency. "As an adult, I can see it wasn't really my fault, but this baby *is*." She covered her bump with protective palms, turning up a face that was so anguished his gut clenched as though he'd been kicked. "She told me so many times that lust was bad and I slept with you anyway. I don't blame you for hating me, but I can't live with the glares and the snide remarks, Zafir. I won't bring my child up in that. There has to be another way."

The ground seemed to shift under him. *Wasn't really my fault, but this baby is…*

"Fern…" He could hardly believe what she was saying. "Is *that* the reason you didn't tell me about the baby? You thought I'd blame you for it?"

"Don't you? You're obviously furious." Her hand came up as she choked out a helpless noise.

"Because you hid this from me!"

She jerked at the sharpness of his tone, but only pinched her mouth into a mutinous purse. "I shouldn't have let it happen. I knew what I was doing was bad."

She was ashamed to have slept with him, but not in the way he'd feared.

It struck him that all this time, while he'd been

remembering the way she'd kissed him with abandon and taken him greedily into her, he'd been forgetting something far more important. *Men don't come on to me. How much experience do you think I have with refusing one?*

Moving forward on feet weighted with self-reproach, he took a seat on the wingback chair that faced her. As he leaned his elbows on his knees, he resisted the urge to tuck the loose tendrils of hair that fell against her cheek behind her ear. He didn't trust himself to let it end there.

And she had no idea.

"Fern, how many people were in that tent that night?" he asked quietly.

She lifted a baleful glance. "I know what I did, Zafir. I remember exactly who instigated this conception."

Her skin radiated with color all the way down her neck. He would bet it went well into that belly and even into the thighs that had clamped around his hips with determination to draw his hard sex deeper into her welcoming depths. Not just offering, but begging. Insisting. She dropped her face into her hands as if she couldn't bear to recall.

While it was all he thought about. Heaven had opened its gates and pulled him inside. He hadn't even tried to resist. Not really.

"I meant to pull out," he stated baldly. "I knew the chance we were taking before I let it go as far as it did." As much as he would love to let her carry all the blame, he remembered precisely the moment when he'd stilled her hips and tried to maintain his sanity. Then she'd said, *I want it to be you.*

He had wanted it to be him. The thought of any man following where he was being invited had been unthinkable. She belonged to him. He remembered the way the word *mine* had echoed in his head as he had breached and possessed and imprinted himself so indelibly onto her body that they were now tied together for the rest of their lives.

"You might have been at your best fighting weight that night, but I could have pushed you away. I'm not a victim."

She shook her head, keeping her face covered. "I knew better. I was reckless and this is the consequence."

"My baby is a punishment?" he asked testily.

She flinched and scowled at him over her fingers. "No. I just mean that I'm no victim, either. I knew what I was doing."

The hell she had.

He rubbed the tops of his thighs, hearing Ra'id's condemnation of him. Accepting it. He never should have touched her.

But he had.

"Maybe we're both casualties of a divine sense of humor, doomed to repeat our parents' ill-conceived actions." He let his brow quirk at his own bad joke. "We made that baby together, Fern. Literally."

She lowered her hands, face red as a beacon, but a light of earnestness glinted in her wet eyes. "Do you really see it that way? Because I'm not blind. I know what a mess this is."

"It is," he agreed. "I'm not going to sugarcoat that part. Right here, the two of us working out what to do, this is the easy part. When we take it out there, it will get ugly. I know that and I'm angry that I'm in this situation, but with myself, not you. If that's the reason you're trying to keep your distance from me, because you think I'll blame you, then stop. Coming here to take responsibility for my child means *taking responsibility*."

She seemed to let that sink in, her body seemingly braced, shoulders set with wary tension.

"Is that all you feel?" she challenged in a way that punched his heart. Vulnerability widened her eyes as she hurried to add, "I mean toward the baby." Her lashes dropped in a way that left claw marks down his insides.

He wished he could offer her love. He was starting to realize she'd probably never known it in any form.

"Because if you just feel a sense of duty..." she continued.

"No, that's not all I feel," he assured her, hitching forward on the cushion, willing to lay himself bare because on this topic, he felt no shame and he thought it might reassure her. Win her over. "The first time I held Tariq, I experienced such a rush of emotion. Something I'd never felt before." He clenched his fist, experiencing again the knock of his heart punching the inside wall of his chest, extending itself outward to try forming a shield around the baby. It reached across the space between them now, trying to take in this new one. "I felt so protective and proud it was laughable, but terrified and overwhelmed, too."

The intense vulnerability had been foreign and unnerving to a man who took for granted his health and strength and power, but he'd grown to accept this feeling as a part of parenting.

"He was mine and I knew I'd stop at nothing to keep him alive and well. There's no word to describe that emotion except fatherhood. I already feel that toward this baby."

Her jaw softened and her expression went misty and soft. "Really?"

"Really. You have to marry me, Fern."

She brushed impatiently at the tears that brimmed at her eyelids. "But I feel so guilty. Mum warned me so many times not to have sex, not to get carried away, and I just let it happen. I couldn't face telling you. I was so certain you'd look at me like she would have. Like I was so *stupid*."

He wondered if she remembered why they'd let it happen.

She sat there, a ball of misery, not exactly encouraging him to believe she looked back fondly on their time at the oasis the way he did.

Which was neither here nor there, he told himself. Marriage was his priority. The rest could be addressed later. Maybe that was a shortsighted attitude given the hurdles they'd face, but he *would* marry her.

"You should pack. If we don't leave soon, we'll be driving in the dark."

"Pack?" Fern was still absorbing the fact that he wasn't pinning all the blame for this pregnancy on her when he made a suggestion that was more of a politely worded order. Her brain emptied all over again.

He smiled faintly. "We'll stay with my grandfather until you're cleared to travel. If that means waiting until the baby comes…" He shrugged.

She felt her world dissolving and pressed her lips together, trying to keep herself in control of her own destiny. "But…" There were too many arguments rising in her to find them and put them in order of importance.

"As comfortable as this flat looks, it's not very secure. Do you even have a real bed here? Or are you pulling a mattress out of that thing?" He pointed at the sofa she perched upon.

She glanced at the blankets she folded each morning and set on the hassock before putting her bed back under these cushions. "Miss Ivy and I do it together," she murmured. "It's spring-loaded, not heavy. Just awkward."

"Well, I don't want you tripping around, rearranging furniture."

"But I have work here. Students who are counting on me."

"You left one teaching job without notice. Surely someone can step in?"

Fern had already talked to a few students about helping them over email or webcam, especially after the baby was born. The library had a modern setup and Zafir was right. Miss Ivy was retired, but she could take over until other arrangements were made.

"I'm not ready to change my whole life," she protested.

"Your whole life has already changed," he reminded her with a patronizing smile.

He was right, but she still scowled anxiously toward the small bureau where she kept her clothes. Her own photo stood upon it, showing her accepting her teaching diploma. That's who she was supposed to be: a middle grade teacher in a quiet village here in the north of England.

"I don't think you know what you're doing," she told him. Had he heard the bit about how she was illegitimate? She knew nothing about her father.

"My first marriage was arranged and we were even less acquainted than you and I. I'm already a father. I grew up the son of a sheikh and an Englishwoman. There won't be many surprises for me in any of this."

Right. His first marriage to a woman he always spoke about with reverence, according to Amineh. Did that mean he was capable of loving a spouse he acquired through an arrangement based on logic? Could he come to have feelings for her?

Worrying her lip, she glanced up to see him watching her and licked where her teeth had made her bottom lip raw, then swallowed as forbidden thoughts crept into the corners of her mind. Would they...?

The consequences of giving in to lust were bad. She was being slapped in the face with them right now.

Come on, Fern, a voice chided in her head. *How much more pregnant could you get?*

But even if he wasn't angry with her, it didn't follow that he *liked* her. While she was in love with him. What sort of future did that set up? Her pulse started to trip into a racing flight and clammy sweat broke out all over her skin. She'd never imagined she would marry anyone, especially a catch like him. This was surreal. He was going to wake up tomorrow and scream loud and long at what he'd proposed today.

He stood and glanced around. "Is there a case somewhere that I can fetch?"

"Can I…" Oh, he looked very tall and dapper and unreachable, standing over her that way. They were the worst match ever. She'd have to make him realize that before things went too far. "Can I just say that I'll come with you and we'll talk more about the marriage idea later?"

"If you want to say that, go ahead," he said dryly. "But we're marrying, Fern. As soon as I can arrange it."

"I really do think you'll regret it, when you've had time to realize what you're suggesting," she insisted.

"Your concern for me is cute. If I had an ounce of chivalry in me, I'd extend the same consideration toward you. Give you more time to talk both of us out of it. But even though I don't blame you, neither of us is going to hide from this. We made a baby. We're going to marry. Then we're going to live in Q'Amara and raise it together."

Fern ruminated in the car, aware that she was being a pushover. Did you call a woman *easy* when she couldn't seem to say no to marriage?

His already having regard for their child had

moved her, she couldn't deny it, but she was letting him take complete control of her life and she knew that was wrong.

Part of her was relieved, of course. His plan would lift some huge worries off her shoulders, like where would the money come from? But she was a fairly independent person. She'd had to be. Emotionally and financially. And the fact was, she might have got to know what he liked between the sheets, she might be certain she was in love, but in many ways, they were still strangers.

"You're sighing a lot," he remarked, gearing down to take the off ramp.

He drove with smooth confidence, not like he had anything to prove, but owning the road regardless. Late winter rain battered the roof and swished under the tires. The wipers slapped at full speed. There was no use trying to listen to music so they'd been sitting in silence since she'd made him stop to let her use the loo at a fast-food place.

"How well did you know your first wife when you married her?" she asked.

There was a pause of surprise, then in a cautious and very neutral tone, he said, "Not well."

If she wasn't mistaken, a thin, transparent, bullet-proof wall had just slid up between them. It was disconcerting and certainly didn't reassure her. It made her think she should leave things at that, but as much as she liked to avoid confrontations, this marriage idea of his needed more discussion before she could get behind it.

"How did you come to choose her? Or…how did it all work?"

He kept his gaze on the road, movements still steady and economical, but a hint of stiffness shaded his voice. "Given the situation with my parents, I knew when I took over that I would have to prove I was more Arab than English." His mouth twisted in dismay.

"The expectation that I would reject my mother and the Western half of my life did not sit well with me," he admitted with a sidelong glance. "We have our differences, but my mother is as much my family as my father. However, I knew that marrying a woman from Q'Amara, *proving* I was not given to blind passion for all things English—" another glance, this one filled with dry significance "—was necessary. Sadira was from an excellent family. Her father was known for his traditional values. Politically, the match allayed many fears that I would try to force change at the pace my father had. The fact that I thinned the foreign blood in my successor helps my approval rating and eases their acceptance of Tariq as my successor."

A small "oh" of apprehension escaped her as she computed that his second child might not be viewed so charitably.

He covered her hand and squeezed with warm strength, pressing reassurance, but also a streak of sexual awareness, through her blood.

"We'll make it work, Fern."

She stiffened in surprise at the way his light touch flooded her with giddy warmth. Should she squeeze back? She was sure that continuing to behave like a teenager in heat would only cloud things. His people expected decorum, for heaven's sake! Not some British nymphomaniac as their First Sheikha or whatever she'd be called.

"I don't see how," she protested, voice made husky by the weight of his hand on hers. "Did you have a happy marriage with your first wife even though you were strangers? Is that why you're so confident we can prevail?"

He removed his touch and draped his hand on the stick, but didn't change gears.

"She knew what was at stake," he said in a level tone. "We both went into the marriage willing to make compromises for the sake of maintaining peace within the palace and beyond it."

"See, Zafir? I can't offer you that! I'm a guarantee of conflict for you."

"My mother never once came to Q'Amara. My father didn't think it safe, but from remarks I've heard over time, her actions were taken as a snub. I am hopeful that your willingness to live there, your acceptance of our culture, will go a long way to smoothing rough edges."

"Yes, well, you have to know it's one thing to take a contract in a foreign country, quite another to adopt one as your home. Especially one so patriarchal."

"We visit my mother two or three times a year. You won't be held hostage there," he said with a twitch of impatience around his mouth. Then, somewhat defensively, he stated, "I know we're behind with women's rights, but change doesn't happen overnight. I have learned from my father's experience to take things one step at a time. And I can't be everywhere, doing all things," he added tiredly, then perked up. "But look at the work Amineh does. You could take up those same causes in Q'Amara," he urged, warming to the topic. "You're bright. A natural educator. I would like that, Fern. I would like that very much."

The suggestion stunned her. She considered working with women to ensure the health of their children. It wasn't bra burning, but it was something everyone could get behind and benefit from. Within seconds, her eager mind was leaping with excitement to get started. And it meant she could be an asset to him, not a detriment.

But the way he said it, like it had only just occurred to him, made her wonder.

"Did your first wife do that sort of thing?" she

asked, already sensitive to wearing the woman's shoes.

"No," he said flatly. Something flashed in his expression, but she could only see his profile and whatever it was gone before she could identify it. "She was pregnant. Tariq was young."

I'm pregnant, she almost said. And Amineh managed a work schedule around having two children.

He must have sensed her puzzlement because he added, "As I said, she was very traditional. Not complacent, but not like Amineh, who was educated here and exposed to different ideas. Sadira wasn't interested in taking a public role."

Sitting deeper into her bucket seat, Fern let that explanation sink in. "She didn't really have time, did she? Amineh said she died of cancer."

"She did." The privacy field he'd erected swelled with thick layers.

"Did you come to love her?" she worked up the courage to ask, even though her trepidation of the answer was so strong her voice shrank.

His jaw worked as he took care to gear down and follow a curve through a gate and into a tunnel of wet, overhanging tree branches down a long graveled drive.

"Love—the passionate kind found in marriage—is a Western notion. Not something that served my father well."

Zafir is more Arab than English, remember that, Fern. Her lungs shrank and hardened, squeezing her heart. *But Amineh has love*, she wanted to argue.

The boulevard of trees ended abruptly and the estate house, gloriously regal with spiking chimneys and a staid façade, struck her in the face. It perched on the highest hillock that overlooked rolling grounds, a pond and, farther in the distance, thick green woods, all of it curtained by a fey mist of rain.

The house itself was intimidating in its sense of peerage, and consisted of ancient bricks and tall windows. The north side was coated in ivy, the south held what she thought might be a solarium. The garage was its own building with seven double doors.

Zafir followed the circular drive around a fountain then parked before the wide front stairs, clicked off the engine and turned toward her while the rain pattered loudly on the roof above them.

"Sadira is Tariq's mother. I love him with everything in me. For giving him to me, I will always have the utmost regard and respect for her. You already have the same from me, Fern."

Meeting his steady stare was hard. She was afraid he'd see the shadows of wanting more in her eyes when she'd never realized how badly she *did* want more until this moment. He expected her to tie herself to him for the rest of her life, cut off any chance of meeting the man who might love her and settle for what was, quite possibly, more than she had ever expected before today.

"I'm worried you won't respect me in the long run," she admitted. "I'm not a good match for you. I don't have a strong personality. You can, quite obviously, talk me into anything," she said with a disparaging gesture at where they were. "I don't want to be a doormat and I don't want to see your contempt as I turn into one."

He frowned, deflating her.

"That puts me in a difficult position," he growled. "If I disagree with what you just said, you'll accuse me of talking you around. Let's do this. Try me, Fern. I've seen you hold your ground. I'll keep in mind that a little defiance is a lot for you and we'll see how far we get."

She snorted and said, "Okay," then rolled her eyes at the irony of capitulating. Again.

He grinned, looking so handsome he made her catch her breath. When his gaze fixed on her mouth, her heart stopped.

A flicker behind him made her nod toward the house through the drizzle-coated window.

"Someone's coming," she told him, reaching for her handbag. Had he been thinking of kissing her? She really would be a puddle of spent willpower if he did.

"Stay there," he commanded as she started to reach for her door latch.

He pushed out of his side and said something to the man who'd rushed out with an open umbrella.

Now would be the time to push back against one of his dictates, but it was no easy task to throw herself from a vehicle these days in a fit of independence. She sat there like a lump and waited for him.

A moment later, while the young man extended his arm to cover them both with the umbrella, Zafir helped her from the car, giving her an illusion of grace as he levered her bulk with a firm but gentle hand under her elbow.

With a murmur of thanks, Zafir exchanged keys for an umbrella and escorted her inside while the servant—was he called a footman?—collected her case from the boot.

Is this it? Zafir had asked when she had only that one case and an overnight bag after completing her packing.

She had a few boxes in Miss Ivy's storage compartment in the basement. "But they're just sentimental things I wasn't ready to part with after my mother passed. Nothing I really need," she'd explained. "I was starting fresh when I took the overseas contract."

He hadn't said much to that, had only carried her things to the car while she'd said her good-byes to Miss Ivy. Fern had lingered to assure her friend that while she didn't know if she was marrying Zafir, she had to admit that he was devoted to his baby and that meant more to her than only another child rebuffed by their father could understand. She couldn't in good conscience keep him out of her baby's life.

Somewhat reassured, Miss Ivy had repeated that she was always there for Fern and now, entering what looked more like a museum than a house, Fern wondered if it was too late to change her mind and go running back to the sofa bed with the iron bar that had dug into the middle of her back every night.

A butler greeted them. At least, that was Fern's assumption of his title when introduced to Mr. Peabody, who bowed and took her coat. He glanced at the footman as the young man entered with her case. "I'll ask Mrs. Reid to prepare a room in the guest wing—"

"Miss Davenport will stay in my suite," Zafir interrupted. "I'll take her there now. Please let my mother know we're four for dinner."

"Of course." Another bow and Mr. Peabody disappeared.

Zafir guided Fern up the right wing of the curving dual staircase to the landing where they were level with the ornate chandelier over the entrance-way. So much space! It was like visiting a posh opera theater, not a home.

Their footsteps made no sound on the thick ivory carpet. They passed ancient portraits and little tables and vases and candle sconces that she had enough history education to assess as Tudor and Regency and Victorian. Old, old family heirlooms.

Zafir was out of his mind, bringing her into this.

His "suite" was essentially a town house, taking up all three floors of the southeast corner of the main house.

"My mother converted it for when my father stayed with us. After he passed, she couldn't bear to be in here so she moved back into her old rooms. Tariq has the upstairs to himself. I don't bother keeping a full staff. We eat in the main house, but there's a kitchen below along with laundry and the rest."

The rest being...an indoor pool? A bowling alley?

"And you make do with this," she murmured, pacing the lounge that could fit a dozen of Miss Ivy's little parlor.

An archway on the left led to an expansive dining room with a balcony that overlooked the *outdoor* pool, covered at the moment. The fading light through those windows was the only natural light into the lounge because, she quickly realized, the front of the apartment was dominated by the master bedroom. Peeking through *one* of the sets of French doors into his private space, she noted that he liked earth tones and modern art and tons of room to stretch. The view of fields and woods beyond the tall windows was breathtaking.

The footman left her case at the bottom of the stairs. His curious eyes glanced off her belly before he offered a quick smile. "Will that be all?"

"Thank you, James," Zafir said.

With a bow, the young man started off, pulling a buzzing mobile phone from his pocket as he went. Glancing at it as he reached the door, he turned and said, "Excuse me, sir. I'm to let you know that Ms. Calloway has arrived. Mrs. Reid will bring her up. She wants to check that the guest room is in order. Also, your mother would like to speak with you."

"Leave the door open for Vivienne, tell Mrs. Reid we're not using the guest room and please inform my mother that I'll be tied up until dinner."

James nodded and hurried off, leaving the door open.

Fern stared hard at Zafir's stony expression. Had he heard her at all in the car five minutes ago? Her nerves pulled taut with anxiety at having a confrontation, and part of her was so hot for him, she didn't even want to fight him on this, but...

"Is this a test? You just told a stranger that I'm sleeping with you without asking me first." She didn't even know if she was allowed to have sex!

He blinked as though her complaint surprised him. "It's a little late to pretend we haven't shared a bed."

"And a little early to start doing it again!"

"What do you...? It's a big bed," he said, going a little darker beneath his deeply tanned skin. "I realize we might have to wait until the baby comes, but where you sleep is not negotiable. We can't make this marriage work if you're haunting another side of the house."

Haunting. Interesting choice of words, but hardly the most pertinent factor here. "But you are expecting this to be a real marriage. With, um, sex and everything." Oh, she hated herself for blushing with anticipatory heat.

He tucked his chin and lifted his brows. "You said you weren't a good match for me, but when it comes to bed, we're inflammable."

She'd love to think that would be enough, but... "There's no guarantee that sort of thing sustains," she argued, crossing her arms. "What if it wears off?"

"Shall we see if it's still there now?" He took a step toward her.

"No." She retreated and hugged herself, trying to contain the bloom of excitement that expanded in her. She could barely think when the prospect of sex with him filled her mind.

He stopped, rooted and still, his posture aggressive, and scowled as he narrowed his sharp gaze into some kind of tractor beam that willed her toward him.

"This is what I mean, Zafir! I don't have any defenses against you, especially physically. Marriage is the biggest decision a person makes. Look where giving in to my hormones has got me so far. Do I really want the rest of my life to be decided by the simple fact that you turn me on?"

"So you don't want to sleep with me?" he demanded.

"I'd like a chance to think about it!" she cried as she finally identified which door led to the powder room and moved through it.

It was as much an escape as to use it for its intended purpose, but she didn't come to any firm conclusions until she emerged to find him talking to an attractive brunette. The woman was smiling and nodding and blinking her thick, darkened lashes with flirty awe at him.

A green monster, warty and equipped with dangerously sharp teeth, rose inside Fern. He's *mine*, she thought, and knew in that second that she was sunk. The idea of him sleeping with any other woman was abhorrent. He had said to her at the oasis that if he couldn't have her, no one else would. Well, if she *didn't* accept him, someone else would. The only way she could ensure he wasn't making love to other women would be to lie with him herself.

Such a chore, she chided herself. But there was an insecure part of her that wondered if they really were still as volatile as they'd been. She wasn't the pristine virgin he'd had eight months ago.

"Here we go," Zafir said, indicating Fern so the supermodel pivoted on her high heels and gave Fern a once-over with a sharp, critical gaze. "Fern, this is Vivienne Calloway, Amineh's stylist."

"I'm delighted to work with you. Please call me Vivienne," she said as she came forward and shook Fern's hand. Her stomach was concave and her hips were the width of a soda straw. Her shiny hair slithered with silky, shampoo-ad brilliance. Her perfect teeth practically dinged as she smiled. "May I call you Fern? Amineh and I are on first-name terms and she has instructed me to pull out all the stops for you."

"Amineh?" Fern repeated, glancing warily toward Zafir.

"I spoke with her while I was loading your things into the car."

Fern's knees weakened. Her hand was still in

Vivienne's warm grip and turned into cooked asparagus. "What did she say...?"

"That you would need something to wear tonight," Zafir answered blithely. "We dress for dinner."

"She suggested the blue dress from her own wardrobe and I agree, now that I've seen you. The color will bring out your eyes. Let's try it on, see if it needs adjustment."

Minutes later, Fern was in a silver slip with a powder-blue lace sheathe over it. The sleeves were a demur three-quarter length, the collar scalloped across her plump breasts. Shoes were another matter, but Vivienne brought a bag filled with a variety of sizes and styles from her car.

"Maternity wear is so tricky, but if you feel comfortable in those, they'll do," she said about a pair of low silver pumps. "We'll have more choices when we're not worrying about swollen ankles. Now lie down and rest while I tailor that dress and set up to do your hair and makeup."

Fern did as she was told, partly out of genuine exhaustion, partly to escape what was happening to her. This morning she'd woken in Miss Ivy's flat, gone to work for a few hours, caught her regular bus and wondered if there was enough of last night's chicken to make a sandwich for lunch. In the last few hours, her entire life had spun into chaos and she needed to be still for a few minutes to let the pieces settle.

She didn't expect to sleep, but crashed hard and woke to the click of the lamp.

Vivienne smiled. "I let you sleep as long as I could. Rest is the ultimate beauty enhancer. But it's time to dress."

Fern submitted to makeup and hairpins and a fitting for a new bra, one in ice-blue lace with matching bottoms that she was thankfully allowed to change into privately. When she looked at the final result, she blinked at the stranger in the mirror.

Her eyes popped like freshly minted shillings from a face where her freckles had been downplayed with a layer of light powder. Her mouth was coated in a shiny nude gloss and her hair was gathered like an Edwardian maiden's with a pearlescent blue ribbon woven through it. She looked as modest as she usually did, but sweetly maternal and, she had to be honest, quite pretty.

When she moved into the lounge, she was both anxious and excited to see Zafir's reaction.

He wore black pants and a white shirt closed at the throat with a black bow tie, and he shrugged on a white dinner jacket as she emerged. He looked her over as he buttoned his jacket, his gaze incredibly thorough, but dispassionate and assessing.

"No?" she prompted uneasily. Behind her, Vivienne was zipping and clipping things back into bags and cases. She'd taken such care and shown such enthusiasm for the result, but maybe Fern was a lost cause.

"Honestly?" he asked.

Bracing herself, she nodded. "Yes."

"Don't cover your freckles. And I prefer your hair loose. But you look very lovely." He moved close to brush his lips against her cheek. Something flashed in his eyes as he drew back. Pride or possessiveness. Maybe both. When he showed her what he was holding, his expression shifted from a hard stubborn set to something less implacable. Appeal. "Will you wear this? Please?"

A ring.

"Oh," she breathed.

"It was my English grandmother's. My first wife wore one that belonged to my father's mother."

Another heirloom from some yesteryear when jewelers were romantic enough to set a blue sapphire in white gold and encircle it with diamonds like petals on a flower. A pair of green stones off either side played the part of leaves.

It was elegant and priceless. Fern could only stare.

"In my country, wedding rings are worn on the right. Do you mind?" He held up his palm, inviting her to place her hand in his.

"Zafir, are you sure…?"

He picked up her hand himself, but just held it as he said, "I can't see into the future any better than you can, Fern. But right now, yes, I'm sure this is what I want. I'm sure *you* are what I want. Do you want me?"

She couldn't lie. Deception wasn't ever easy for her and right now, with him standing so close and looking at her like she meant something to him, she couldn't be anything but completely honest.

"I do," she whispered, and reinforced her agreement with a shaky nod.

His breath came out in a light caress on her knuckles and he smiled with arrogant satisfaction, but what looked like relief, too. Like she'd made him happy.

His touch as he threaded the ring onto her finger and kissed her knuckle sent a thrill of joy through her. Maybe he was right. Maybe they could make it work.

CHAPTER EIGHT

ZAFIR WASN'T USED to feeling anything less than wholly confident. He wanted to take heart from Fern's willingness to accept his ring, but the way she'd talked about not having any defenses, especially physically… Did she think he would force her? Not in a million years! He hadn't pressed his first wife—

But then, he hadn't felt a need for her like he did for Fern. Was he above seducing her? Clearly not.

Her balking at agreeing to sleep with him bothered him. Not in an arrogant, entitled way. In a deeply disturbing way. Even before he'd found her and confirmed her pregnancy, he'd been unable to shake the near irresistible urge to fetch her back into his life. Sleep together. Make love to her one more time.

A storm he'd barely acknowledged had been crashing inside him for months as he fought those urges, only settling when he'd had her in the car beside him. Now a fresh turbulence kicked up, despite the flash of his grandmother's ring from the hand that gripped his arm as she steadied herself on the shiny oak floor.

She had reservations about resuming intimacy with him and he supposed he couldn't blame her. He'd promised hc wouldn't cause her to lose her job or get pregnant and that vow had been thoroughly shattered. If she'd rather have a platonic marriage while she learned to trust him again, he should be prepared to accept it, but he found it wasn't something he could face easily.

Glancing pensively at her, he saw only a bundle of cascading red curls held in a blue ribbon.

"Chin up," he said, refusing to let her hang her head before his family. "Neither of us will be apologists for making a baby out of wedlock."

"More like poster children," she commented under her breath, surprising him with her levity. "I was looking at the pattern in the parquet. This house is beyond words."

It was a country cottage compared to the palace in Q'Amara, not that he said so aloud. The staff would put rat poison in his dinner if they overheard such a remark. But she did make him see things with new eyes.

"I think you'll be good for me, Fern," he told her as they arrived at the music room door. "You remind me not to take things that I value for granted." He held her gaze with a significant look.

Whether that reassured her at all, he wasn't given an opportunity to judge. Peabody opened the door to exit the room with an empty tray and stepped back as he saw them, allowing Zafir to enter with Fern.

Her grip on him tightened, betraying her nerves. Soft greens and old gold leaped at him. He took in antique furniture and silk area rugs that he did take for granted, along with the cheery fire beneath the white mantel and the green-and-gold drapes that closed out the blustery night. This was, in many ways, the happiest place of his childhood since it was where his family had been whole.

The two people waiting in tight-lipped silence weren't happy. His bringing a woman into the house was unusual. His accommodating her in his private quarters was eyebrow-raising. Her pregnancy, well, there was a reason his mother had wanted to speak to him upon his arrival. She was always the first to smell scandal and in spite of her personal history, maybe because of it, she was always the first to try smothering any flames that threatened to disgrace the family again.

His grandfather sat in his favorite wingback chair. He wore a dark suit that set off the gold chain of his pocket watch. Zafir's mother wore a long black velvet skirt and a starched white blouse. The flouncy ribbon at her throat was the only bit of softness in her elegantly aged demeanor. She had not broken when Zafir's father died. She'd hardened like carbon placed under extreme pressure.

His grandfather betrayed no surprise at seeing either of them, even though Zafir's arrival at the house had been as unannounced as his guest's.

"What is that infamous quote by that American ballplayer?" his grandfather asked rhetorically. "Something about déjà vu all over again?"

Zafir's mother snapped a look to her father and brought it round to her son, keeping it as sharp as an ice pick. "It would be nice if I could learn certain news directly from you, rather than through the servants," she stated.

"They told you I was engaged? How did they know when Fern only accepted my proposal a few minutes ago? Grandfather, Mother—my fiancée, Fern Davenport."

Zafir provided their titles, but as his mother offered her hand for a reserved handshake, she said stiffly, "William and Patricia, please," and found her Lady-of-the-Manor smile. "I see my daughter has replied to my call with a message after all. I was told she was indisposed." Her gaze slid down the dress Fern was wearing. "I remember now where I heard the name Davenport," she added condescendingly.

"Your granddaughters spoke of me?" Fern said, pink beneath the layer of powder on her skin, but earnest, which was appealing in its particular way. "I've missed them. I hope they're well?"

His mother's expression flickered with indecision, as she tried to determine if she should soften or not. "I didn't talk to them long. I was distracted, but yes, they're quite well. Taking some sort of dance lessons."

"You know the girls?" his grandfather asked. "Forgive me for not rising. Gout."

"Fern," Zafir offered as he turned a chair from its place near the fire so she could sit.

She thanked him with a smile and lowered into it, then answered his grandfather. "Amineh hired me last year to tutor the girls in English. I lived with them for about six months."

"Really, Zafir," Patricia said in an undertone meant only for him. "The governess?"

"It's a bit late for snobbery about who we make our children with, isn't it, Mother?" Zafir replied in a conversational tone loud enough to make Fern pinch her lips together.

"Are we speaking openly then?" his mother asked, metaphorically dropping her gloves. "Because I have to wonder if you did make this one."

"Don't take offense to that, Fern," Zafir said

without breaking eye contact with his mother. "It's a family tradition. My grandfather said the same thing to my father."

Fern might have gasped. His mother definitely did.

His grandfather leaned forward to admit to Fern, "It's true, I did." Ice rattled in his glass as he lifted it with a palsied hand and tilted it at Zafir's mother. "All three of my girls were highly sexed. Zafir's father wasn't her first."

"No, your solicitor was," Zafir's mother declared with a very fake, very tart smile.

"We'll have a paternity test when the baby is born if it will set your mind at ease, but I'm quite confident it's mine," Zafir said. With false geniality aimed at his mother, he added, "You'll have another grandchild. I thought you'd be delighted."

His grandfather snorted. "Heard that one before, too. I hope you're proud of yourself," he said to his daughter, raising her ire even further.

"How is this my fault?" she demanded, elegant and composed, yet indignant. "I didn't get her pregnant."

"No, but you were after Amineh about schooling the girls in English."

"*Here*. I wanted her to put them in school here. Not hire someone—" She glared at Fern.

Fern sat very still, body language braced and watchful, hands a tight knot in her lap.

Zafir was sorry to put her through this, especially when his mother was lobbing some heavy artillery and Fern was already sensitive to being blamed, but he wouldn't have the strong personality he did possess if he hadn't grown up holding his own against the ones who'd raised him.

"She did it to please you," his grandfather pointed out before Zafir could interject, indicating Fern with his half-empty glass. "This girl never would have been under his nose if you hadn't interfered."

"That's funny," Zafir said with a snort.

"It is *not*," she retorted frostily. "And even if I do bear some responsibility for her hiring someone, you ought to know better than to let an opportunist—"

"Talk to Ra'id before you decide who took advantage of whom, Mother," Zafir interrupted, leaning a hand on the back of Fern's chair. "Fern's virtue was his responsibility while she was under his roof and he failed to preserve it. He's barely speaking to me right now."

Fern looked up at Zafir, her brows tugged into an anxious crinkle. "Really? He's not upset with me for being a terrible example for his daughters?"

"Their grandmother is a terrible example for them," he stated, enjoying it. "But no, partly he's taking advantage of the chance to get back at me for all the years I was so protective of Amineh, but he knew exactly how worldly you were. He is genuinely offended with me and remorseful toward you. Expect a sincere apology when you see him next."

"That's not necessary!" she insisted, chin crinkling as she tried to hold a wobbly smile. "I'm just glad they're not cross with me. I'd love to see Amineh and the girls again."

"She's anxious to see you, too," he assured her, moving his hand so his knuckles felt the tickle of her curls as he brushed them back from her shoulder. "I should have explained when I said that we come here a few times a year, Amineh and I try to overlap our visits. If she doesn't come to us in Q'Amara first, we'll—"

"Zafir," his mother said sharply. "You are not actually marrying her. What happened to the marriage you were arranging with that troublemaker's daughter?"

"Ra'id has suggested his cousin would be a better match for the girl," Zafir said, straightening. "As a personal favor to his family, I have stepped out of the running. My real motives will be obvious after our marriage is announced," he told Fern. "But it's a very good alliance for both sides, he's closer to her age, and it still provides the girl's father some of the influence he craves.

By facilitating it, I hope to defuse some of his animosity. My hope is that it will turn out well."

"You hope!" his mother repeated. "That doesn't mean it will. That doesn't mean you should marry—I'm not being a snob," she remarked to Fern. "My sister married a male nurse, of all things, so I understand that spouses come in all vocations."

"At least she married him," Zafir's grandfather said in an aside, proving that pretentiousness came in all sizes in this household.

"Well, I couldn't marry, could I?" his mother snapped with such vehemence it took the temperature to arctic levels. "Everything we worried could happen, *did*. Do I wish I could go back and marry him? *Yes!* But we'd all be dead now if I had. So no, Zafir, you may *not* marry this English woman. You won't stir it all up again and leave me sleepless here, terrified every time the telephone rings. You'll live here, Fern," she said firmly. "I realize I've said some things that might have put you off, but you're a mother. You understand our instincts to protect our children. That doesn't go away no matter how old or pigheaded they get." She tossed that last statement at Zafir. "And you've seen how private the southeast unit is. We won't be in each other's way. I would enjoy finally having one of my grandchildren so close."

Zafir half stepped so his leg was right up

against Fern's chair. He had expected resistance to his marriage because Fern didn't have a pedigree dating back to Elizabeth I. Not *this*.

"I'm not here to ask permission, Mother."

"It's denied regardless." His grandfather finished the last of his drink and set it on the table with a decisive *clack*. "Your mother will be worried sick, Zafir. How can you even consider doing that to her again? And the baby? You can't put it in harm's way. Amineh's situation is different. No. Marry this girl, I agree you should do that much, but leave her here."

"No. *Don't* marry her. It makes you a target—" Patricia said, voice rising, but Zafir spoke over her, even louder.

"You two are not keeping my wife and child away from me." His hand went to Fern's shoulder. He felt her start at his touch and firmed his grip on her, dimly aware he wasn't being reassuring but snarlingly possessive. His mother's anxiety could frighten Fern off.

"We're not keeping anyone *away* from anyone," his mother said crossly. "I wish you and your sister would stop acting like your father and I were denying each other access when it was a necessary arrangement that worked—"

"It didn't work for me!" Zafir boomed so ferociously his sharp words echoed into the silence it created.

His mother went white and she looked away, chin thrust out.

Zafir realized his body was primed for a physical altercation, blood racing, muscles twitching with readiness. It wasn't just the split in his psyche that had prompted his outburst. His broken family was an old fight, but Fern and his baby were *his*.

His grandfather hitched forward on his chair, obviously finding it a struggle, but his voice was strong. "Zafir. Your father and I didn't see eye-to-eye on much, but I never doubted his love for your mother. He wanted to take her to Q'Amara with him. It wasn't safe. He had to leave her here and he couldn't even marry her. It was too much for your people to take. He had to keep her like a damned mistress. *You* were meant to be with him when he was killed. I won't let you put us through that again. She—" he pointed at Fern "—stays *here*." Then he pointed at the floor, his tone that of a man still confident in his position of power despite his physical decline.

"Do you think I would risk my wife and child if I thought that same danger existed?" Zafir demanded aggressively, but the word *love* gave him pause. Love had made his father weak enough to take up with a woman that his country had never accepted. It had weakened him in the eyes of the people he governed and had weakened him as a man, prompting him to take ridiculous chances and make bad decisions.

What was he doing if he took Fern back to Q'Amara? Was it a wise decision? Or a selfish one? Why was he so determined? Lust? Or something else? If you cared about someone, you put their interests, their *lives*, above your own.

His mother rose to pull a tissue from a box on a side table. "Was it *so* horrible to live in two places?" she challenged in a choked voice, keeping her back to them as she dabbed at her eyes.

Tortured by his inability to grasp his own motivation, Zafir did what any child did under stress. He went to his mother. Taking hold of her shoulders, he set his chin alongside her hair, sorry he'd caused her to cry, but… "If you had thought there was a chance you could have lived together, wouldn't you have tried?"

They would have, he knew they would. They had loved each other very deeply, which had formed the trade-off for the difficult decisions they'd had to make. He wasn't prepared to make those same decisions. *He needed Fern with him.* Now that he'd seen it as possible, no other option was good enough.

"Oh, I hate when you sound like him sounding like he knows he's right," she said as she brushed his hands off her shoulders and swiped impatiently at her face.

Disturbed, feeling as though he didn't quite know himself, Zafir gave her time to compose herself by moving to help his grandfather to his feet. When he offered a hand to Fern, she kept her eyes downcast.

That shook him. If she refused to come with him, he didn't know what he would do. Seduce her? Talk her around? Demand?

Leave her here after all?

Gently tilting her chin up so she had to show him the reflective silver of her eyes, he said, "I would not take you anywhere that I thought would risk your life, Fern. I hope you trust me in that."

"Childbirth notwithstanding?" she said with an ironic quirk of a smile.

He didn't laugh. Couldn't. What *had* he done to this woman?

"That was a joke," she said.

"It was a rebuke for being careless with you and I deserved it," he said, dismayed. Furious with himself. He brooded through the entire meal.

Much to Fern's relief, Zafir ended the meal by stating they would take after-dinner coffee in his suite. The minute the door was closed behind them, she asked, "Did you do that on my behalf? Do I look as exhausted as I feel?"

"*I'm* exhausted," he countered, eyeing her pensively. "Jet lag is catching up to me. But my grandfather tires easily these days and you have had a long day." His mouth twisted with self-disgust. "I'm sorry to have put you through all that."

"I had a nap earlier," she reminded him. "I'm tired, but it's more social fatigue. I feel like I was in the longest job interview of my life. Would you mind?" she asked, showing him where the zipper of the lace sheathe closed at the top of her spine.

"My grandfather liked you," Zafir said as though trying to offer a comfort.

"Who is Esme?" The old man had accidentally called Fern that for the second time right before Zafir had cut short their post-meal chatter.

"My grandmother. You don't look anything like her. She was quite short, had black hair and eyes like mine, so I thought for a minute he'd had one too many whiskeys, but I think it's your manner that made him think of her. She was quiet and thoughtful the way you are. The rest of us are scrappers, determined to jump in ahead of everyone else and take control. She was always an influence of calm, taking time to think about things before she reacted." He released the zip on her dress and his light touch sent a ripple of pleasure through her.

"I'm not calm, I'm terrified," she admitted.

"About coming with me to Q'Amara?" He touched her shoulder, urging her to turn to face him.

"I meant in general, but..." His mother's anxiety had been contagious. The whole time she'd been answering questions about where she grew up and who she knew through Miss Ivy and when she was due, she'd been thinking about where Zafir expected her to sleep and what her future with him might hold.

A firm kick nudged her from her absorption into a light gasp and a touch on the spot where the baby was insisting more space was needed.

"Are you okay?" Zafir frowned at her belly.

She chuckled. "As far as personalities go, I think we've created another scrapper. Quite pushy," she pronounced with rueful affection, liking what he'd said about his family and how he'd intimated she had a place in it that was notable and valued.

"Can I...?" His gaze fixed on her belly and his hands came up. He hesitated as he looked to her for permission.

Her nerves jolted like an electric shock had run through her, pushing a flood of tingling warmth into her inner thighs. He hadn't even touched her!

The strength of her anticipation startled her. Her life had been fairly devoid of human contact before he had taught her how wonderful it could be. Since then, especially in the last few months, she'd discovered some people loved touching pregnant women. Strangers asked to pat her belly.

Sometimes they didn't even ask, but this was different.

This was Zafir. She had been aching for his touch since forever. And it was his baby. Emotions, already amplified by pregnancy, threatened to overwhelm her.

"I— Of course," she said huskily, quivering with tension like liquid at the rim of a cup. She lifted her hands and waited.

At first he barely grazed her with splayed fingertips, like she was a soap bubble that would burst at the least pressure. The thought made her lips twitch and she covered his hands, showing him how to press firmly enough to find the baby's shape.

"That's the bum. And this is where—oh! Did you feel that? Must be a knee, right?"

He choked a breath of laughter. "Doesn't that hurt?" He explored gently where the nudge had happened.

She shrugged. "Not really. Takes me by surprise. Keeps me awake sometimes. I honestly don't think either of us will get much sleep if I—"

"Shh." Discovery of magic played across his face. "It must be so strange," he said with quiet reverence, shifting the lace on the silk of her slip as he moved his hands around the shape of her belly. "Can you even wrap your mind around it? That's our child that we made, right there. I can feel it, but I can hardly believe it. Are you scared? About the delivery?"

"Yes," she admitted, giving him a crooked, sheepish smile. "Not that I have anything to be frightened of specifically. Just apprehensive, I guess. I've read too many books on what could go wrong and keep worrying what will happen to the baby *if.* And Miss Ivy—" Wait. Would he…? "Do you want to come into the delivery room with me?"

He stopped moving his hands, but left them resting on her. His brows tugged up in surprise. He parted his lips without speaking, like he didn't know how to respond. "It didn't occur to me— Yes, I do," he asserted firmly before a rare glimmer of uncertainty entered his eyes. He searched hers. "Do you want me to?"

"I do. Very much." So much it made her head swim. Her hands found their way onto his and held him there. "I didn't even think about it until just now and…I would feel so much better if I knew you were there to make it all go well. Please come with me."

"Of course, Fern." His smile wasn't steady, but maybe that was her eyes, blurring with relief and joy. "Of course I'll be there." A shaky laugh rattled his voice and he sidled his hands up her waist to where she was more Fern than baby, his touch possessive and tender.

This was how it was supposed to be with a man when you were having his baby. She was going to burst, she was so happy right now.

"But aren't there classes or something?" he asked. "Men are pretty much useless, I suppose. Nothing to know except how to stay out of the way, but I should learn that much, shouldn't I?"

Fern laughed. "Miss Ivy was going to them with me. But didn't you go in with your wife when she had Tariq?"

He let his hands fall away, leaving an impression of coolness where his hands had been. "No. She opted for full anesthetic and caesarian section. But her specialist is world-renowned. I'll—" He pinched his lips into a frustrated line. "I'd like to call him and ensure he can take you on, if you're cleared to travel."

It was hard for him to back off a step and not tell her what he would make happen. She probably wouldn't have been able to hide her smile over how hard that was for him if she hadn't heard the greater question in his statement. He was asking if she was coming to Q'Amara.

The mere fact that he was leaving the door open for her retreat was incredibly reassuring. She genuinely didn't think he would risk her life or that of his baby and something else was niggling at her. His wife had *opted* for surgery. She wanted to know more about that and his marriage in general.

She wanted to know Zafir better.

It was not something that could happen if she was haunting a different house in another country. And she'd seen tonight how the division in his family still affected him. She couldn't bring herself to do that to him. To their child.

She nodded. "You should call him," she agreed. "If I can travel, I think it would be good to have the baby there. So there's no question of citizenship."

He nodded slowly, with more than agreement. Pride. His smile wrapped her in a blanket of approval. Cupping the side of her face, he caressed her cheek with his thumb. "This is going to work, Fern."

She hoped so. She dearly hoped so.

Zafir was ready to find his mattress.

Last night had been painful in the best possible way. Without any further debate, Fern had slipped into his bed while he was on the phone, leaving him to find her there.

It had been like Christmas morning—a tradition his mother had insisted upon despite his father's Muslim faith. Zafir had stood for a long moment admiring the ribbon of her red hair, the polka dots of her freckles, the hidden potential in her slumbering countenance.

Eventually he'd gone in search of something to

wear to bed. He went naked under most things whether it was sheets, *thobe* or tuxedo so a simple pair of boxers was a struggle to locate. Then he'd dozed beside her, too aware of her to fall into a proper sleep, mind turning over possibilities while his body ached to pull her across the desert plain of sheets into the pillar of his own.

She'd been equally restless, getting up several times.

"I'm sorry I keep waking you," she'd murmured when she'd come back at one point. "Do you want me to sleep somewhere else?"

"No. I could find another bed if I wanted to." He'd rolled toward her, cursing the expanse of the mattress. "Does your back hurt?" He'd done some reading before settling in.

"No, there's just no room in this body for anything but baby anymore." She'd yawned, and added in a drowsy whisper, "I keep getting so confused. I wake up and realize you're here and think I'm at the oasis so how can I be pregnant? But it's nice to sleep with you again. I missed you."

She'd drifted off, leaving him thinking, yes. For all the ache of desire coursing through him, it was very nice to have her beside him. He'd missed her, too.

They'd then had a busy morning of appointments and arrangements. Fern was given a complete physical before an official came in to marry them in a perfunctory ceremony witnessed by his mother and grandfather.

His mother could grouse all she wanted about a proper church wedding, but the one thing his father had got right in Q'Amara's evolution was tolerance of other faiths. Zafir was often criticized for not limiting or outright censoring online content, but his mixed parentage meant neither of the two dominant faiths in his country felt threatened that he would refute one or the other.

Which is why he'd chosen a civil union rather than favoring one religious blessing over another.

They'd followed it with photographs for the press release and he'd approved his mother's preliminary guest list for a proper reception in the summer. They'd eaten in the air on the way to Q'Amara before Fern had gone to sleep in his stateroom, leaving him answering emails between fielding conversation attempts by the obstetrics nurse he'd hired to travel with them.

He had timed the release of their marriage announcement so it hit the wires just before they landed. His country's media stations were barely out of bed and no international paparazzi were among the lenses trying to get a shot of his new wife. Well veiled in the predawn light, she didn't offer much to scoop for those who'd made it to the airport in time to catch them deplane and travel to the palace.

He ought to sleep now, he knew, before the demand for interviews became too great to ignore and he was tied up for hours.

But sleep was not the reason he wanted to find his bed.

No, after the brief research on his tablet last night, he'd lain awake with a need for confirmation burning a hole in his mind. He'd waited through Fern's exam with barely controlled impatience, was heartened to hear her pronounced in excellent health and well enough to travel with sensible precautions, and then Dr. Underhill had thankfully been ahead of him.

"And since I expect any groom in your situation would want to know, Zafir, I'll save you the trouble of asking. Fern, so long as you feel comfortable making love, it should be perfectly safe to do so."

She'd blushed crimson, of course. Zafir had deflected the conversation to boring topics about transferring her file to the specialist he'd contacted to take her in Q'Amara. He hadn't said a thing about Underhill's remark afterward.

But when they'd kissed to seal their marriage, he'd quested for a response and she'd opened as beautifully as desert flowers to rain. He had been quaking inside with wanting her ever since, like a volcano threatening to crack under the pressure of burning lava rising within it.

If he could have locked out the world and seduced her, he would have. But even though he shouldn't ignore the interview requests, there was one task, one person, he absolutely could not disregard.

"Where is she?" Tariq asked as he charged into Zafir's private apartment and looked around the empty lounge.

Zafir had left Fern here, suggesting she put her feet up while he fetched Tariq. He'd had quite the father-son chat with the boy before they'd circled back along the second-floor landing to Zafir's rooms.

The drawback to having an exceedingly mature and intelligent child, Zafir was learning, was the inability to pull any wool over the boy's sharp brown gaze, even when it meant reflecting a less than admirable light on himself.

You told me before that we were born into families of influence and should never misuse that. Did Miss Davenport know that she didn't have to be nice to you in that way, if she didn't want to be?

I believe she did know that, yes, Zafir had claimed, even while a part of him still squirmed under the knowledge that his sophistication and experience well surpassed hers. He might not have coerced her, but he'd taken brazen advantage of her artless joy in discovering passion for the first time.

And was going mad with wanting to do it again.

While she was acting very quiet. His one query, when he'd seen her turning his grandmother's ring around on her finger and asked if she was all right, had been met with a rueful smile. "As you pointed out last night, I like time to consider things and haven't really had a chance to sort through all this. Yesterday I was going to rent a flat around the corner from Miss Ivy and raise this baby alone. Not everyone operates at light speed the way you do," she'd teased lightly.

Which he didn't think had been meant as a warning that he should put the brakes on his libido, but he'd taken it as such. The guilt he was carrying over thrusting her into this new life was enough to instill some worry in him when they arrived in his rooms and she wasn't there. Amineh had been anxious to have a webcam conversation, but Fern wasn't in his adjoining office at his desk or even in the small powder room off that.

His massive bedroom, which anyone could get lost in, was empty. She wasn't behind any of the marble colonnades, wasn't in the vast canopied bed, hadn't entered the dressing room, wasn't sitting in the reading alcove and hadn't walked into his small sunken library to peruse his antique books. The sauna, not recommended in her condition, was empty, as was the bathing pool and the grotto shower with the faux waterfall. She hadn't walked out to his private balcony or followed the stairs down to the pool, either.

Disquiet began to creep into his psyche as he called for her and she didn't answer. Vaguely he was aware of Tariq calling for Miss Davenport as he ran from corner to corner, but Zafir was far more concerned about her condition than maiden names versus married.

"She probably went to her room in the harem," Tariq said with snap of his fingers, chuckling as if they should have guessed that first.

Tariq opened doors that Zafir used so seldom he'd forgotten they were there. A piece of modern art sat in the alcove before them, half blocking the ornate wooden panels, but Zafir's mother had never lived in this palace and Tariq's mother had certainly never come through them. About once a year, Tariq grew curious enough to wander through them and staff cleaned all nooks and crannies of the palace regularly, but otherwise no one entered this wing.

Pushing through with his son, Zafir feared he had the answer to Fern's level of comfort with lovemaking if she'd taken herself into this private domain.

The passage from the sheikh's quarters was short and dim, lit only by narrow slits in the door where it terminated onto a balcony that extended in a circle around the courtyard below, not unlike the main entranceway to the palace.

Unlike the front foyer, it looked down on a communal bath sunk into the lower floor. A glass dome in the roof allowed sunlight to pour onto the tropical plants that were mostly self-sustaining, provided he kept the pool filled and the fountain running. In the four corners, antique gilded cages hung silent, awaiting exotic birds.

Doors led off the surrounding walls into luxurious accommodation reserved for the women in the ruling family: daughters, sisters, mothers. Wives.

Zafir did not find his wife in the opulent suite closest to the shortcut to his rooms, the apartment reserved for Wife Number One. She answered Tariq's call and stepped out to wave from the furthest room, the one traditionally used by the groom's mother. *She* didn't need to sleep in close proximity to the sheikh.

Sadira had chosen and modernized that distant apartment, Zafir had seen after her death, adding a computer desk and a television console along with a contemporary queen-sized bed. The other rooms still contained the sumptuous, pillow-covered mattresses and silk wall hangings that had been refurbished and replaced for their marriage party eleven years ago. Was it significant that Fern had gravitated to Sadira's room?

She didn't look at him as she came toward them. A wide smile for Tariq brightened her face.

Vivienne was not being shy about spending his money on outfitting his pregnant bride, and was doing so very prettily. Fern wore the dress in a silvery moss color that she'd flown it, but her yellow cardigan, abaya and veils were gone. Her low heels clicked on the marble and even though she wasn't as willowy as when he'd first seen her, and her bump sat high and prominent, the rest of her was so curvy his mouth watered. Her loose hair bounced and shimmied. As she moved into a beam of sunlight, it caught glints of gold and auburn, producing a halo effect, making Zafir catch his breath at how utterly stunning she was.

"Tariq! It's so nice to see you." Her genuine warmth wasn't even for him, but filled Zafir with gladness.

Tariq canted his head at her. "You look...different."

"I'm sure I do," Fern said, cutting a glance at Zafir that sent him a private message. He hadn't been aware of a desire to become one of those couples who read each other's minds, but he liked the sense they were.

"Has your father talked to you about, um, why I'm here?" she asked, one hand resting with light significance on her belly.

"Yes. And I wanted to know, do you expect

me to call you *Mama*?" Tariq asked in his forth-right manner. He crossed his arms and hitched his hip in a way that Zafir recognized was his own stance when he had already made up his mind about something, but had to suffer through propriety before he could get to the bottom of things.

Fern's expression blanked. "Oh. I hadn't…"

"*Yes,*" Zafir interrupted firmly.

He had thought he'd covered everything with Tariq and leave it to his son to ferret out a fine point, but Zafir found himself loving the idea of Tariq using the title. Fern, at least, would live up to the designation. She already valued Tariq for everything he was.

Fern's expression flickered and her smile was vaguely apologetic toward Zafir before she returned her attention to Tariq.

No. A cold hand clutched around Zafir's heart and his pride began to tear down the middle as he realized Fern was going to contradict him. She would *not* reject his son.

"I would be honored to know you thought of me as your mother, Tariq," she said with quiet sincerity, and he gave himself a mental shake. Of course she wouldn't reject the boy. "If your father would like you to introduce me as your mother and call me that in public, then please do. But it would mean more to me if, in private, it was something you chose to do. If…" Fern sent another contrite glance toward him that, Zafir realized, was an apology for challenging his dictate. "If your father doesn't mind, I'd prefer that you think about it and decide on your own if you'd like to address me as Mother. Until you're certain, perhaps you could call me Fern?"

And she thought she didn't know how to get her way, Zafir thought with a quirk of private humor.

"You make a good point," Zafir allowed, so profoundly relieved it was easy to be magnanimous. He wasn't used to being gainsaid, but now was as good a time as any to demonstrate to both of them that he would always be willing to take Fern's opinions into account. "Fern it is, unless you feel differently," he said to Tariq.

"That's not what I meant," Tariq said with an exasperated roll of his eyes. "I meant do I have to say *Mama*. It's so babyish. I'd rather call you *Mother*. I can't call you by your name. That would be too confusing for my little brother or sister. And disrespectful."

"Yes, I suppose it would be," Fern said, pinching her lips together in a poor attempt to suppress a laugh. "Then yes. I would be delighted if you'd call me Mother. If you're sure."

"I'm sure," Tariq said with offhand confidence. "I don't remember my mother and I like you quite a bit. I was very disappointed when I visited my cousins and you weren't there," he declared with a pointed look. Then he transferred his attention to Zafir. "May I call my cousins and tell them Miss Davenport is my mother now?"

"You may text your uncle and ask when would be a good time to have that conversation," he said. "Then you should get back to class."

"Will you take over my lessons?" he asked, turning back to Fern.

"I think I will be busy with the baby very soon, but I will always take an interest in your studies. Please ask your tutor if I could sit in sometimes, particularly for language or history, so I can learn, too."

Tariq nodded and started toward the wide archway of the main passage back to the palace. He checked himself and came back to give Fern's expanded waist a befuddled search, arms half-raised for an embrace.

"Oh, um—" Fern bent awkwardly, accepting Zafir's quick grasp of her hand so she didn't lose her balance. Tariq's arms went around her neck and he landed a quick kiss on her cheek. She closed her eyes, mouth pressing into a smile of deeply touched emotion.

"I'm really happy you're my mother," Tariq said, making Zafir's heart swell with pride. "My cousins will be so jealous," he added with an impish grin and raced off.

"Oh," Fern said, placing a hand over her heart. "I didn't expect that."

"The kiss or the part where he treated us like half-wits?"

She laughed, glanced at the marble floor and tucked her hair behind her ear. "The part where he made me feel like we're a family. I never had that. It means a lot."

The glitter of happy tears on her lashes filled him with the impulse to cradle her close. Sex? Yes, he wanted to fondle and caress, push into her and know the exquisite clasp of her again and again, but this desire was more than that. He wanted to feel her against him, smell her hair, bring her into his life as much as his home.

How had she come to mean so much to him when he'd only known her a little over a week last year and not even two full days in the last forty-eight hours?

She caught his eye, read something in his face that made her bashfully turn away and move to the low wall of the balcony, where she followed the curve of the nearest staircase with her eyes, leaning to study the benches and broad-leafed plants surrounding the pool.

"This place is incredible. Can you imagine what it was like— When was it built?"

"Five hundred years ago. And yes. As a teen I stood in this empty wing more than once and fantasized about exactly how incredible it must have been." He could still manifest the pictures he'd created in his mind: the abundance of naked breasts and bottoms, the mysterious configuration of a woman's body that he'd only barely understood, yet longed for the authority to command for further study.

She giggled as though reading his thoughts.

He moved closer. "But my days of valuing quantity over quality are gone," he assured her.

She blushed and retreated toward the stairs. "Are you sure? There are an awful lot of rooms here, looking ready to be filled by women of every shape and size."

"Is that why are you're in here?" he asked, moving to descend beside her, one hand clasping her elbow in case she lost her footing on the worn, slippery steps. "Are you checking up on me? Ensuring I'm not hiding anyone?" Or scoping out a residence for herself? His muscles hardened with tension.

Culpability flashed in her eyes. "I didn't realize where I was going when I started snooping. But isn't this where I'm supposed to be? Why are *you* here? Isn't it forbidden? That's what *harem* means, doesn't it?"

"Most Westerners think the word means *brothel*." He liked the slant of her smile. If he wasn't mistaken, she was flirting with him, but very shyly. Because she had so little experience with it, he supposed. He probably volleyed back a little too hard when he stated arrogantly, "I'm the sheikh. Nothing in this palace is forbidden to me."

She blushed, no match for his suggestive tone.

"These rooms are for the children?" she asked, peering into an alcove with sleeping benches around three sides. It only had a curtain, not a door.

"The children of wives—yes, plural," he confirmed at her look, "stayed with their mothers upstairs. Girls moved into their own space as rooms became available. Boys left the harem around six or seven. I moved Tariq when his mother died, since there was only his nanny to keep him from falling in the pool in here."

"Then all these little rooms were for servants?" she asked.

"Concubines and eunuchs," he explained, thinking with affectionate amusement, *so naive.*

"Oh. Of course." Her cheeks pinkened. Her expression grew more speculative as she peered into the spare accommodations with new eyes, making her way back toward the corner below where they'd come in. "This one's quite spacious," she remarked, stepping into the biggest room on the ground floor.

"Reserved for the sultan's favorite. You'll notice that aside from the Number One Wife, she has the shortest distance to walk to be with him." He pointed to where the stairs ended near the passageway to his chamber. "And all who visited him had to pass the wife's door."

"Politics are not a modern invention, are they?" she remarked, moving deeper into the concubine's lair. "She had air-conditioning," she said with surprise, studying the window of latticed marble that stood behind a waterfall that ran in his front courtyard. Glittering light bounced off the gold plate behind him to brighten this space more than the other rooms.

"One resident of this room was so prized, the most trusted eunuch slept beside her so she wouldn't be murdered by the other women." He stalked closer to her, fully sympathetic to his ancestor's beguilement.

Something wistful passed over her face. Her lashes fluttered as she realized how close he was. She tried to make her retreat look casual, but that's what her quarter turn and step away was.

He'd been chasing her around the harem long enough.

"Fern," he said quietly, keeping her from walking out of the room altogether. "We should talk about what the doctor said. About making love."

She stopped, but didn't turn. Her hands moved

to clench together and her upper arms stained with an extensive blush. "Do you want to?"

A sudden pang of juvenile fear hit him. He didn't want to admit to his feelings before she did. He might be staring down his first marriage all over again. But if trust was an issue, the only way to gain hers was by being completely honest.

"Do I want to talk? Or make love? I'm prepared to wait until after the baby, if you're not up to it, but yes. I would like to make love to you."

"Even though I'm fat?"

"You're not fat. You're beautiful," he said with sincerity that bordered on reverence, moving closer. "Is that why you're hesitating? You're feeling self-conscious?"

"Yes," she said in a small, overwrought voice. "And because feeling this way seems so brazen in my condition."

A laugh of relief started to rise in him, but was knocked back into his throat by her next words.

"And so sinful if it's just lust."

CHAPTER NINE

"Not that I expect you to love me," Fern hurried to add, afraid to turn and see how he was taking what she'd accidentally blurted.

But it was hard to say those words when it might be true that she didn't *expect* his love, but she yearned for it. As she'd turned his grandmother's ring on her finger in the car on the way here, taking in the way her own life had revolved into something completely unexpected, she'd realized there was only one reason she would allow it to: *love*.

She loved him so much. It wasn't a surprise. She'd known she did, but somehow she'd convinced herself it wouldn't sustain. Like such an intense feeling could wear off. It hadn't. She was carrying his baby and had held him right in the space between her heart and their child's the entire time she'd been apart from him. Her love had grown with each passing day, just as their baby did.

"Fern."

She could hardly bear the careful way he said it, like he was treading into very delicate territory.

"It's okay," she insisted, telling herself it was. "We barely know each other. When have we had time to really talk?" They'd been too busy trying to bite back their cries of pleasure. She covered where her cheeks ached, they went so ruddy and hot. "And we're married now, so it's not really a sin to feel this animal attraction, but is it enough? Was it enough for you and your wife?"

"*You* are my wife," he said forcefully. Then his chest expanded as he drew in a long, deep inhale, his expression closing her out. He indicated the door and the stairs that began right outside them.

Fern deflated as she climbed alongside him, sorry she'd brought up his first wife when it was so obviously a sore subject. Warm feelings would never grow between them if she alienated him.

Rather than open the door to the passage to his bedroom, however, he touched her elbow to draw her into the quarters closest to it.

"This is where Sadira should have slept if not with me."

Fern had glanced in here when she began her explore. She'd been taken with the round bed and its red quilted headboard and silk canopy that reminded her of their tent in the oasis. The suite had a beautiful modern bathroom along with a sitting room of Ottoman furniture and a private balcony. It was screened even though it only looked over Zafir's private courtyard and pool. She supposed the small room off the side would have been used for a nursery.

"I said the other day that because she gave me Tariq, I would never speak a bad word about Sadira. I meant that." He glanced sideways at her while he stood in the door and looked diagonally across the harem to Sadira's old rooms.

Despite his *thobe* and *gutra* and constant air of command, she sensed a kind of despondency in him. Powerlessness.

"She allowed her father to talk her into marrying me for the good of the country. I thought she felt as I did. That it was an advantageous match and that we had enough respect and liking to form the foundation of a strong relationship."

"I feel like you and I have that," she felt compelled to say, instantly concerned. "Don't you?"

His expression flickered across to her with fierce pride. "We have a hell of a lot more than she and I did. One of those things…" His gaze fell to the floor before he turned to face her. His gaze brooked no hesitations or prevarications. "Fern, does it bother you that I'm only half-English?"

Taken aback, she could only say, "No! Of course not. I barely give it any thought." He was Zafir, so sexy and striking she walked around dumbfounded that he'd ever looked twice at her. "It's only something I worry about from the side of, you know, the politics. Those things your mother worries about. Obviously it would be nice if the whole world could get over bias and never exclude someone for skin color or other superficial reasons. I kind of wish *I* wasn't English. If I was Arab, I could help you instead of being a problem."

"Don't wish yourself something you're not," he commanded with a twitch of cynicism. "Especially when you can't change the circumstances of your birth any more than I can. I couldn't remove the English part of me and Sadira had no use for it. In fact, I have come to believe, she felt soiled by having anything to do with me."

"What? No!" Fern denied.

He cast her a look that was both disparaging of her naiveté and deeply shadowed by old hurt.

"You really think so?" she asked softly. Cautiously.

He ran a hand down his face. His reluctance to confide was plain in the time it took him to form a response.

"She refused to sleep with me. Barely spoke to me. After she gave me Tariq, she kept to her wing of the palace and, I have come to fear, left her cancer undiagnosed because she saw it as her only escape."

"That's— No! But you have divorce here. Don't you?"

"She wouldn't have asked. Divorced women are looked down on as having done something wrong. And she'd already lowered herself by marrying me."

"How could she think like that?!" Fern couldn't even comprehend such a thing.

"Because of what I was. Illegitimate with tainted blood. Birthing Tariq was her duty and she fulfilled it, but when I say she gave him to me, I mean it. It was like he had contaminated her. She didn't breastfeed him, didn't care for him. I changed him and gave him his bottles along with the nanny."

She found herself shaking her head, the new mother in her feeling the cleave in her heart at the thought of anyone rejecting a helpless infant. "Amineh said you always talk about her like you loved her—"

"Amineh has no idea. No one does," he said with a snap of impatience. "Do you think I want Tariq to know his mother felt nothing toward him? Reviled him as much as she was repulsed by me?"

Fern's heart broke for the boy and the man. "Oh, Zafir. I'll never breathe a word to him, I swear." She would, in fact, do everything in her power to be the mother Tariq should have had.

"But I can't believe anyone would look down on either of you for anything, especially something you couldn't help!"

He said nothing, only stared back into the harem, jaw pulsing with tension, brooding.

"So you didn't even try for more children? You love Tariq so much. I can't imagine you not wanting more."

He choked out a laugh, following it with a pained pinch of the bridge of his nose.

"I couldn't bring myself to try. Our wedding night— It was awkward, obviously. We didn't know each other. She was a virgin. I thought she was just bashful. I did everything I could to make it nice for her. I stopped more than once, aware she wasn't responding, but she insisted..."

He dropped his hands to his sides and closed them into fists, swallowed, his mouth a line of disgust. "I thought the second time might be better, but I felt like some kind of monster. It was just wrong. I wound up leaving before we were even naked. I couldn't work out where I'd gone wrong. I carried that. I agonized for weeks. Just when I found the nerve to talk to her about it, she turned up pregnant and made it clear there was no need for me to touch her again. She delivered a boy and, aside from one night when Tariq went into hospital with a bad fever, never offered herself to me again."

"What do you mean. She actually came to you…? What did you say?"

"I asked her if she wanted another child. She said no, and I said I hoped he would be fine. He was."

"She sounds so mean," Fern breathed, hurting for him. Here were the shades of suffering she'd seen in Amineh that she'd thought Zafir too strong to feel, but of course he felt it. He was just better at hiding it.

"I don't think she was capable of sexual feelings for me. There is a lot of prejudice in this world and I was subjected to it from both sides of my life. I know what it looks like and that's what it was. She was pressured to marry me for my position and her father's political gain. She saw herself as a martyr."

"Zafir, I'm so sorry." She went across to him, setting a light hand on his arm. "I can't believe anyone would not see what a remarkable man you are and feel privileged to be near you."

His face spasmed with emotion. Hooking his arm around her, he pulled her in close, one hand crushing into her hair as he pressed his mouth to her temple for a long moment.

She closed her eyes, overcome at the poignant sweetness of his embrace, for once not sexual, but emotional. It felt healing. Loving.

But the effects of his proximity were there, too.

She was aware of his torso beneath the familiar, thin fabric of his *thobe*, the scent of cotton and man, the humid air and the musical tinkle of the water below. It all pulled her into the sensual spell that was Zafir. Her blood began to heat and her skin prickled into receptiveness.

Self-conscious at her instant response, she started to draw away.

"Don't," he murmured and made her tilt her head to look up at him. "Given everything I've just told you, you must realize how important it is to me that you feel physical desire for me. Don't hide it from me. Even if all you feel is lust, Fern, I'm glad it's there."

She struggled to hold his gaze, certain her true feelings were painted all over her face. He was too astute and experienced not to see the signs.

"It's love," she whispered, feeling worse than naked. Like her soul was exposed. The agony of having no defenses left against him at all twined through her voice. "I think it happened at the oasis. That's why I was so afraid to tell you about the baby. I couldn't bear for you to hate me when you'd seemed to like me a little—"

"A lot," he amended, cupping her face in two hands. "Ah, Fern." His face spasmed with great pain. "I fell in love, too. And I couldn't admit it even to myself. Not when it made me just like my father."

"I'm s—"

He set his thumb across her lips, stilling them. "*I'm* sorry that I wasted months when we could have been together. I thought I should be able to control my feelings, especially if it was only lust, but I couldn't. I *can't*. You're everything I want, the only woman I think about."

"Oh, Zafir…" She went up on tiptoes, trying to kiss him.

He groaned, hands closing into her hair as his mouth landed on hers, rough and hot.

He gentled immediately, groaning again, but didn't release her. With a growl of apology and frustration, he tenderly ravaged her mouth.

She closed her eyes, falling apart at the sweetness of having his kiss again. His arm came around her back to haul her in. Her hands closed on his *thobe*, grasping and trying to pull him into her. She couldn't get close enough. Silly bump in the way!

He moved them deeper into the room, kicking the door shut with a slam. As he pivoted to sit on the padded love seat, he dragged her onto his lap, knees on either sides of his thighs.

"Okay?" he murmured between consuming bites of her mouth, his hands riding her skirt up her thighs and then cupping her bottom proprietarily, fingering under the lacy edges of her undies.

She braced her forearms on his shoulders, kissing and kissing him. Running fingers up the back of his neck into his hair. Knocking his *gutra* askew. Reuniting. "I'm too heavy on you," she gasped, but couldn't make herself pull away. His hands wouldn't let her.

He laughed, using his nose to nudge her chin up so he could kiss her neck. He'd done that sort of thing in the tent at the oasis, told her without words what he wanted. Her throat, her collarbone, her breast. She scraped her hair back and away, offering. She told him with the angle of her body where she wanted his nibbling kisses, and sighed when he found the exact spot that melted her into heaven.

She ignited in his arms. Absolutely burst with the thrill of feeling him, smelling him, returning to this amazing place where touching and kissing and caressing was perfect and right and necessary. Where it was an expression of more than sexual attraction. *Love*.

Trying to wriggle closer, she scraped at his back, demanding the *thobe* come off, but he was sitting on it. He tried to set her on her feet and lift her dress at the same time.

"No, I'll be too self-conscious," she protested. "The lights…I just wanted to see and kiss you…" She slid to her knees on the area rug and pushed at his *thobe*, exposing his legs, running her hands up the rough hairs on his thighs.

With a savage noise, he stood long enough to pull it off and away, then sat and tried to bring her back up onto him, but she stayed on the floor and ran her fingers to the tops of his thighs, staring.

"I've never seen you," she murmured, sending him a shy look before letting her enraptured gaze fall back onto his naked, aroused flesh. He felt so familiar in her hands yet looked darker and more imposing than she'd pictured.

He swore, but let his hand fall to the armrest. The other one gripped the backrest behind him. "Look then. But I'll want to do the same and then are we really doing this? Because I love you and I want to show you how much."

She stroked him, coming up on her knees to lean forward and breathe across his taut skin. She looked up, almost asking for permission.

His eyes narrowed, intense as the blue-green at the center of a flame.

Smiling with a woman's wicked delight at having mastery over her man, she drew him into her mouth

He hissed and threw back his head, arched to press deeper against the swirling caress of her tongue. "I won't last," he said through his teeth.

She gave him an approving hum.

He held out, though, making sounds of deep

torture while he grew harder than titanium under her ministrations. Her inner being soared with confidence at knowing he liked this, but more than that, she loved knowing it meant something to him that she wanted to give him pleasure. She expressed her love this way, openly and without reserve.

"I'm watching you," he told her in a voice that tightened her skin. "I've only felt you do that in the dark, but you're loving this, aren't you?"

She let her smiling eyes meet his, allowing him to see how much she enjoyed giving him physical pleasure.

He was flushed and fierce, his possessive gaze barbaric, but his caress on her cheek was tender as he made her stop. "Are you comfortable? Kneeling there like that?"

"I…yes," she said dazedly. "I don't want to stop."

His mouth widened in a feral smile. "Good. Neither do I. Stay where you are."

He rose, but set a hand on her shoulder when she would have pushed up on her knees.

"No, keep your elbows on the cushion." He lowered behind her and ran his hands under her skirt, bunching it until it sat under her breasts. Then he slid her knickers down her thighs.

"You want… Like this?" she asked, staring with scandalized eyes at the impression he'd left on the cushion between her clenching hands. "Maybe if the lights were off—" she protested.

"Lift your knee, *ya amar*." Her underpants were whisked away. His hand stroked her naked thigh and smoothed over the curve of her buttock. "Freckles everywhere," he chuckled softly. "I feared I would never know for sure. Are you as aroused as I am?"

They both gasped as he caressed between her thighs where she was slippery and aching. She dropped her face into the cushion, stifling her moan of yearning.

"No." He continued to stroke her while he tangled his free hand in her hair, tugging just hard enough to pick up her head. "Let me hear you. We don't have to bite our lips anymore."

"Someone will come."

"We both will," he assured her smokily.

"It's too much," she whispered, growing taut all over as her climax approached.

"I never told you how good it was that night," he said as he shifted to lean over her. His naked body brushed the exposed skin at the backs of her legs, her bottom and the small of her back. He rubbed his shaft against her sex in a way that was deliciously familiar and not enough. Not anymore. Not now she knew how it felt to have that thick pressure inside her. "You took me apart with your heat and tightness. You're so wet for me again. You make me insane with desire, Fern."

"Don't tease, Zafir," she begged. "Please."

He was shaking as he entered her, passion barely restrained.

She cried out, pressing back to make it happen faster. Deeper. She was shattering and he was barely touching her, sliding his hand around to caress her as he made gentle, shallow thrusts.

He pinned her right on the cusp of climax and held her there. She arched, letting her moans of enjoyment fill the room, clutched in a storm of such magnificence she could only shudder and release ragged cries of joy. It was intense, her orgasm so close that when he decided they were ready, it arrived, swift and powerful. She feared she wouldn't survive it, but didn't care, crying out with abandoned ecstasy.

Dimly she was aware of him holding himself tight and deep, biting through her dress at her shoulder. His fist covered hers on the cushion and crushed her hand as he convulsed, bathing her in heat, inside and out. They were like a star exploding, so perfectly attuned they were one being melded soul to soul as the waves of climax overtook and drowned them, taking a long time to recede and let them come up for air.

His body branded her where his damp skin adhered to hers. She became aware of him braced over her, still shaking. His heart was pounding against her back. Her own pulse was trying to find a resting level along with her lungs. She remembered what they'd sounded like, how guttural his shout had been over her abundance of ragged cries.

She blushed.

He chuckled and kissed the back of her neck, then stroked her hair off the side of her face with a trembling hand. He touched his lips to the side of her face. "Okay?"

"Just trying not to die of embarrassment. That was rather…" She didn't have words.

"It was," he agreed with a nuzzle of her ear. "Worth waiting for."

She turned her hand under his, wanting to link her fingers with his, but he picked up her hand and kissed the backs of her knuckles before carefully withdrawing.

She settled onto her hip, still trembling, not sure where to look as she attempted to regain her modesty, trying to tug her dress into place and not reveal that as satisfied as she was, she was also still aroused and responsive.

He leaned back on his hand, his other wrist propped on his bent knee. He ran his gaze over her, possessive and impenitent. He was gorgeous. Sexy and comfortable in his nudity. The light gilded his skin to warm polished oak. The way his mouth relaxed in a smile of smugness and his eyelids blinked with heavy satisfaction sent a ripple of warm delight through her.

"You look like a sultan who just enjoyed his concubine," she teased, pleased that she felt confident enough to say it, even though she couldn't help primly tugging her dress into place under her bum and down her thighs.

"Someday I'll be a duke," he said, leaning forward to run his hand up her leg and under her skirt. "One who compromised the governess. I'm starting to think I'll have a harem after all, full of intriguing women who all look like you."

She leaned forward to steal a kiss, but wrinkled her nose at him. "Don't remind me. Your abundance of titles intimidates me."

"Anytime you're daunted by me or any part of this life I've dragged you into, I want you to remember what you do to me. I'm utterly at your mercy. In lust and so deeply in love…" They kissed, tenderly and lingeringly.

"And it's not sinful."

"Not in the least. We're blessed…"

EPILOGUE

Two and a half years later

ZAFIR'S STRONG ARM hooked around her and dragged her from sitting on the edge of the mattress, where she was debating between two bathing suits, to half-under his powerful body.

"What are you doing?" she scolded in a whisper, as if she didn't know. "It's broad daylight."

"Freckle inspection," he whispered back, beginning to unbutton her shirt.

She giggled and combed her fingertips against the beard scuffing his cheek, thinking of the reason he'd given her when she'd asked once why he was so entranced with her spots.

They remind me that there's no clean line between my English and my Arab halves. I'm an aggregate of both, sifted together into one man.

She'd melted, loving him all the more when he made her feel like she was the absolute most right woman for him.

As he trailed kisses between her breasts and she crooked her knee against his hip, already warming with delicious slithers of arousal, she blinked at the tent ceiling above and marveled at the life she had, wondering how she'd come to deserve it.

He lifted his head to give her a puzzled look. "Did you go somewhere? Because making babies takes two, you know."

She smiled, always amazed at how attuned he was to her. "Just having a moment of awe that we ever met. Here of all places. We could have met in England, but no, my soul mate was in a protected reserve that only a few select people are allowed to visit."

"I like to think I would have found you no matter where you were," he said, opening her top to admire her bare breasts. "But I'm glad it was here. Do you know when I think it happened for me? When I was such an ass to you and you were only trying to help that girl. I felt like the lowest form of life. Sick with guilt. Couldn't sleep."

"So you came to my tent, you wicked sheikh." And the girl was fine. She'd just been here with the tribe for five days and they'd all left a few hours ago. Fern's challenge now was figuring out how to encourage girls her age to pursue their education rather than marrying before they were out of their teens. And carefully, because the Bedouins had been instrumental in her acceptance by the rest of Q'Amara. She didn't want to offend them.

Speaking of offended, Zafir was giving her a pointed look. She would have to think about work another time.

"You would have gone away that night, but I didn't have it in me to let you," she recalled, sidling her hand up the sleeve of his *thobe* so she could shape his bare shoulder.

He shifted to settle over her more purposefully. "I like to think I would have left, but I'm glad you didn't test me." He obeyed the urging in her touch to lower his head and kiss her properly.

She had to stifle a moan, it was so good.

"There she is," he said with heated approval, as he cupped her breast and thumbed her nipple, inciting delicious tension in her belly.

They were in perfect synchronicity now. She hooked her calf across his lower back and lifted into him—

The boys' voices approached. "Mother, are you in there?" Tariq called.

Zafir drew back with a beleaguered sigh, expression ruefully disgruntled. "Excellent timing, as always."

She snickered and sat up to quickly button her

shirt, cheeks hot as she called, "Yes, we're here, Tariq. What do you need?"

"Ahmed wants you." A shadow loomed against the front of the tent and separated as their two-year-old son slid off their twelve-year-old's back. Little hands made indents on the nylon as Ahmed's stern little voice said, "Mama. Come."

"I'm coming," she assured him, wrinkling her nose at her husband as she pushed off their low bed to open the front of the tent.

"Baba!" Ahmad said as he spied Zafir, running right past Fern to scramble onto the bed and tackle his father. He looked just like Tariq except for having Zafir's green eyes and what everyone agreed was Fern's pert mouth.

"Oh, yes, I can see it was me he was anxious to see," she said, sharing a grin with Tariq. He was approaching the age where his shoulders were filling out and a light shadow stood on his upper lip, making her so proud of the man he was growing into, yet so wistful at how quickly he was growing up.

"He and Sadiq were fighting over the orange shovel again," Tariq said with a long-suffering shake of his head. "He was angry when I tried to give him the red one. Started looking for you and wasn't happy when he realized you weren't still there."

The toddler cousins gravitated to each other

like puppies in a pack, but scrapped for the sake of it, Fern sometimes thought. "Do you want to leave him here?" she asked.

"No, I'll wait until he's ready to come play again." He moved to hitch his hip onto the foot of the mattress, laughing when Ahmed rose from vanquishing Zafir to growl and attack him. Tariq caught his little brother and pretended to be overcome, falling onto his back on the mattress beside Zafir.

A wrestling match ensued, one Fern stayed out of as the two boys took on their father, making Zafir laugh so hard he weakened long enough for them to nearly overpower him.

"You could help," Zafir scolded her in the middle of it, but she only shook her head, chuckling at his situation.

"I'm Switzerland. I don't take sides," she claimed, and it was true. She loved them all equally, each for the wonderful person he was.

When they tired and settled, Tariq held out his arms to his little brother. "Should we go find Sadiq?"

Ahmed nodded and Tariq sat up, offering his back. Ahmed clambered onto him, pudgy arms closing around Tariq's neck. He bounced, and urged, "Go Sadiq. Go!"

"I'm glad you're having fun with him, but you don't have to spend all your time minding him," Fern said, giving in to her mother's need to smooth Tariq's hair as he came even with her. "It's your vacation, too. I know your uncle wants to take you into the desert with the falcons."

"I know. But he told me that if you and Baba have time alone, you might think about giving me another little brother. Or maybe a sister."

Oh, good heavens. Fire climbed Fern's cheeks as she realized what Tariq—what *Ra'id*—was implying. She looked to Zafir.

He was lounging on an elbow and drawled, "Your uncle said that?"

"He asked me if I wanted more siblings. I said I would so he said I should give you time to think about it and talk about it. If Baba doesn't mind, I'd especially like it if you gave me sister," he said to Fern. "We both would, wouldn't we, Ahmed?"

"Sadiq!" the toddler insisted.

"That's not how it works, Tariq!" Fern blurted.

"I know how it works," he said with a rascal's grin, hitching his brother higher on his back before walking out. "I'm just saying."

Fern clapped her hands over her cheeks as he left, staring into Zafir's laughing eyes. "We're not fooling anyone, are we?" she asked in an askance whisper.

"Apparently not." He hooked his arm behind his head and beckoned to her like the man he was: a sheikh wanting to lie with his Number One Wife, patting the mattress where he wanted her. "So zip the tent and unbutton your shirt. Let's finish making another oasis baby."

* * * * *

LARGER-PRINT BOOKS!
GET 2 FREE LARGER-PRINT NOVELS PLUS
2 FREE GIFTS!

HARLEQUIN®

Romance

From the Heart, For the Heart

LARGER-PRINT BOOKS!
GET 2 FREE LARGER-PRINT NOVELS PLUS
2 FREE GIFTS!

HARLEQUIN®

super romance®

More Story...More Romance

ReaderService.com

Manage your account online!

- Review your order history
- Manage your payments
- Update your address

*We've designed
the Harlequin® Reader Service
website just for you.*

Enjoy all the features!

- Reader excerpts from any series
- Respond to mailings and special monthly offers
- Discover new series available to you
- Browse the Bonus Bucks catalog
- Share your feedback

Visit us at:
ReaderService.com